YEOVI

20.

BUBBLES

BUBBLES

Peter Prince

BLOOMSBURY

'The Carnival is Over'
Words and Music by Tom Springfield © 1965 Springfield Music Ltd
Warner/Chappell Music Ltd, London W6 8BS

First published in Great Britain 2000
This paperback edition published 2001

Copyright © by Peter Prince

The moral right of the author has been asserted

Bloomsbury Publishing Plc, 38 Soho Square, London W1D 3HB

A CIP record is available from the British Library

ISBN 0 7475 5351 3

Typeset by Hewer Text Limited, Edinburgh
Printed in Great Britain by Clays Ltd, St Ives plc

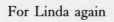
For Linda again

One

I

On his way home from the undertaker's he called in at the Safeway on Streatham High Road. He planned to do the big shop for the week, even though it wasn't a Monday, the day on which for the past few years they'd always done it, having connected rather belatedly the facts that (a) weekends were the busiest times at the supermarket and; (b) being largely unemployed (or retired as they liked to call it before other people), they had no need now to confine their shopping to those days. Every day was a weekend now for them, if they liked to look at it that way. Or another way: one day was much like any other. So they had fixed on Monday, for no particular reason. But not this week. This week Monday had been taken up with her dying.

Long before that – for her cancer had been slow and unhurried in its spread, content to wait for years in the sure knowledge of its eventual triumph – they had had the brave conversations about his solitary future. How he was to conduct himself, how not to give way to gloom, how to find an interest, take evening classes, meet another woman. Shopping, and all things connected with shopping, had cropped up often. She had a set of rules and recommendations that for a time she seemed almost frantic he should learn before it was too late. Watch out that the vegetable compartment in the fridge wasn't left so long that its contents turned into a stinking, slithery mess. Check the sell-by dates on all packages. Take advantage of any special offers that came through the letter-flap. And make sure he kept up the Monday 'big shop' tradition. He was to promise he wouldn't leave it always to the last minute and a dash down the road to the petrol-station shop to scavenge among its sparse and expensive stock of tinned goods. He was to buy healthy food. Vegetables. And fruit. Lots of fruit.

These conversations – edgy, earnest, punctuated with appalled laughter – came to an end quite suddenly. Vincent wasn't sure why exactly, and never did ask his wife her reasons. For himself, he thought it was because of a growing sense that he was only mouthing back to her the clichés he had picked up reading women's magazines during his Wednesday and Friday mornings at the public library. There was always at least one article in them about that sort of thing. Dying, parting. 'Farewell My Husband, My Lover' he remembered one story was called. He'd read it mainly to find out if it was one and the same person who was being farewelled. (It was.) But whatever they were called, the flavour was always the same: profound, sane, courageous, all that. Another rich source of bullshit on the subject he found were the TV movies that he watched at home in the afternoons. Somebody was always dying in them too, somebody else being brave and saying farewell and looking steadily towards the future. In between spasms of shrieking American panic and grief. None of it corresponded with what he actually felt in those last months. Which was . . . boredom. Irritation. Wishing it wasn't happening. Wishing it was over. Being sorry he was wishing that. It was a pain in the arse altogether. Sorry for her too of course, for her supremely, but . . . so much for him to do. And more and more towards the end. The business with the bathing. Brushing her teeth, combing her remaining hair. And then with the shitting and all of that. The last day and night she had been terribly restless. Her hands had groped and pushed and pulled at the covers of the bed in which she lay alone. He slept downstairs on the sofa now. But he had been with her physically during the moments in which she had died, thank God.

By the vegetable counter Vincent bowed his head. An old woman muttered crossly as she had to reach past his inert form to get at the tomatoes. When he could move again, he bought fresh celery, watercress, spring onions and carrots in memory of his wife.

At home he stacked away his purchases, then cut open two sesame-seeded Vienna rolls, smeared the insides with Marmite, added the watercress, and took the tray into the sitting room. He started watching a black-and-white Korean War film, but fell asleep long before Gregory Peck's unit took the summit. He woke in darkness, confused, groping. Knocked over the cup of tea he'd made to wash down his lunch. Luckily it was almost empty. He switched on the sofa-side light. Screwed up his eyes to read his watch. Nearly eight. Damn. He would have great difficulty falling asleep again tonight. Worse still – he remembered suddenly that he had a job to do tomorrow that he really ought to be wide awake for.

From below came a steady industrial thumping which told

him that his downstairs neighbour was home from work and enjoying his music as usual. Like so many, Rodney was still in thrall to the musical tastes he had developed in his teenage years and, unfortunately for Vincent, that meant in his case the era when bands like Aerosmith and Whitesnake ruled the world. An amiable, dreamy-looking young man, who smelled a little, not unpleasantly, of pot, Rodney had some sort of job with an environmental foundation. He'd shown great concern when he became aware at last that there was sickness in the house. Had toiled upstairs often to offer his help, to go shopping, or take out their wheelie bin, or wash the upstairs windows, anything the Stablers needed. And he had a list of healers and shamans and alternative death counsellors for their consideration as long as his arm. Which were all refused of course.

'Is there *nothing* I can do?' he would ask beseechingly when Vincent met him coming in or out of their shared front door. Yes, turn down your fucking music, you heavy-metal freak! Vincent wanted to yell. Haven't you ever heard of noise pollution? But he couldn't do it. Hadn't the heart to. The goodness and kindness shining in Rodney's eyes were too manifest for him to abuse him as he wanted. Besides, Vincent had a deep memory of his own principled battles waged against his parents for the right to play his Little Richard records at the correct ear-splitting volume. It was true that he had been fifteen then, and Rodney was in his late-twenties and damn well ought to know better . . . but still he supposed it was the same good fight, and it would make him a hypocrite to actively join the other side.

Still he had dreaded the thought that Bubbles should

spend her last moments on earth with the sound of Rodney's turgid vibrations in her ears. Fortunately the noise, which penetrated so fluently the floor between his apartment and the Stablers' sitting-room, seemed not to have the power to rise any further. Up in the top bedroom she was safe enough. Only Vincent, twisting and turning on the sofa, was open every night to the assault. But in fact, by some sort of feral instinct, Rodney evidently became aware that the moment of death was getting close, for on the last two nights of her life his CD player was eloquently silent. And then for a couple of nights after.

Presumably Rodney – or one of his death counsellors – had now judged that the period of mourning should be over. Normal service was to be resumed. Still lying prone, Vincent vowed that his own time of truce would also be drawing to an end. With wrathful glee, he plotted his future course of action. First the curt note drawing Rodney's attention to the state of affairs: 'which presumably you are unaware of'. Then a visit or two downstairs. Vincent would be restrained but steady. Implacable. And not afraid to let the edges of his anger show around his reasonable discourse. Then, if necessary, the council would become involved. The London Borough of Croydon. Department of Noise Control. With powers to evict and confiscate. Oh, yes.

II

Meanwhile the pounding continued as before. At last Vincent raised himself from the sofa. He went into the kitchen with thoughts of making himself something to eat. He drank a glass of water instead. It was quiet in here. In truth, by some acoustical freak, the only space on his ground floor that Rodney's music really affected was the living-room. Rather than bringing discord into the house, it would be sensible perhaps for Vincent to make changes in his own layout. He had thought about turning the small room along the corridor into the living-room. At the moment he was using it as a sort of study-cum-overflow from the clothes closets upstairs. He went to have a look. Switched on the overhead light, and surveyed the room from the door. It was certainly a small room. But if he could put the sofa there. And the TV over there where the desk was . . .

Very small room. Nevertheless – he stepped inside – Rodney's rubbish was only a faint, ignorable pulse in here. Like the heartbeat of a young child. Or somebody dying. He went quickly to the desk. Sat before it. Switched on the desk lamp, and the old Apricot computer that he and Bubbles had liberated from her office immediately after the 1983 general election. He loaded the file. It took for ever. At last it appeared on the screen. He began to scroll through it. Page after page. He had been working on this thing for many nights past. As if in anticipation of the public indifference that her death would meet, he had set himself to write Bubbles' obituary. While she was still alive, he had taken frequent breaks from her bedside to come down here and set down the story. Well, her death had come at last, and indeed had gone unnoticed, except for a measly couple of paragraphs in the *Guardian*. And even these were crammed full of misinformation. It was not the case, for instance, that she had been given her nickname on account of her 'infectious smile' and her 'irrepressible sense of humour'. In fact that had started as a sneer by Baz Jacobson, their bitterest Militant enemy in the constituency, and was meant to make fun of her then new hairdo, a big mop of tightly-permed curls, a white version of the Afro, popular in the Seventies. However, because indeed the name fitted some aspects of her personality – yes, all right: the infectious smile, the sense of humour – it spread widely thereafter, and finally even her family, with Vincent the longest to hold out, learned to call her that. To Bubbles' own satisfaction, it must be said, for she had never much liked her real name. And it was her luck that the nickname never achieved wider currency in the press, where it might have damaged her political standing, for it had already been taken by another public figure, a newspaper proprietor's plump and effervescent and highly-visible wife, also since deceased.

Anyway . . . Anyway this thing now shimmering on the screen in front of him had grown far beyond an obituary. In fact, it was useless for that purpose, he knew. Had known really since his first session working on it, when he had filled twenty pages with urgent outpourings. No newspaper would ever contemplate using this torrent. But by then he was no longer bothered with that. Her life, all she had meant to him, to others, could not be confined to a few paragraphs. If the audience for this production was only himself after all – and he had a sneaking hope that at least one day her sons too would read it – then still it was valid, and must be done.

The real problem was, Vincent thought, as he scrolled

backwards now through the file, that after so many pages he had not yet actually got around to dealing with his wife. He had found it difficult to locate exactly where the story he wanted to tell began. And when he thought he had found it, the next time he looked that seemed all wrong, and he'd had to start again, earlier. Which was not even the greatest of his difficulties. For he found that however much he set himself to writing upon his chosen subject, other topics kept pressing in upon his attention, distracting him from the main task. He had meant to write the story of Bubbles Stabler: wife and mother and above all – news and obituary editors please note – a figure of the Seventies, Eighties, and a bit of the Nineties, quoted, profiled, admired, derided. In a small way, a symbol of her time. But instead such strange fish kept rising from the ocean depths. Goldy Stern, for instance. And all those other people: Ivor Trasker and Val, Rob and Tim of course, and Matty, and French Henri and Johnny Blake and Black Nick Gobelins. And the students.

And Russell. Above all Russell. Truly it began with him, Vincent knew that now. As to how it would end, he didn't know. He hadn't written that yet. So many electronic pages used up and he wasn't even close to it. He reached the beginning of the file. Perhaps it was there after all. The end in the beginning, the beginning in the end, all of that. Still seeking guidance from the text, he started scrolling slowly forward again. So many errors of fact, he noticed this time. And so many inconsistencies. (Certain large inconsistencies in his assessments of Ivor Trasker, for instance.) They would all have to be fixed and made good some time, he supposed.

Once he looked up from the glowing screen. It was late

now, and very quiet, apart from the machine's companionable hum. He wouldn't trouble himself to check, but he knew if he went into the living-room it would be as silent there as everywhere else in the house. Rodney would be in bed by now. He got up early to go to his job, came in late. A hard worker, Vincent ought to be able to forgive him his small amounts of recreation, however deafening. The night was warm. Early November and it felt even muggy. But that was how it was nowadays. April felt like June, November like September, and there was hardly winter any more at all. He opened the window beside his desk. The mild air poured in on him. Tomorrow morning he was due to get on a couple of buses and go to speak at that school. Which promised to be quite a farce. Meanwhile, he had to get through the night.

It pierced him suddenly that she would not know this night. This particular balmy night. And all the other nights of his life, she would not feel the air upon her skin, nor ever look up at the skies as he was doing now. Stars over Norbury. Even though most of them could not contend against the dazzle of London, a few could still be seen shining down upon Bubbles' late home. He began to count them.

Two

I

I first realised that my older brother Russell was rising above the ordinary run of South London villains and hard men on the autumn night in 1971 when he brought the man called Goldy Stern to my home. It started no different from any other visit. Russell used to show up late at night at my place quite often in those days and usually with a friend or two in tow. I lived then in a small flat on the Fulham side of Putney Bridge, about equidistant, in an indirect sort of way, between the clubs and pubs and casinos of Chelsea and the West End where Russell and his pals liked to go for their weekend entertainment, and the south-of-the-river boroughs where they mostly lived. So my address had become, as one of Russell's cronies had put it to me once, a regular old piss-stop on the way home.

(Though the number of times it happened made me a little curious. Some of those full bladders, I thought, could just about have made it all the way home. I figured many of these visits were only so that Russell could keep an eye on me. I joked about it with him once.

'We shouldn't keep meeting like this.'

We were standing in the hallway. In the nearby toilet one of Russell's pals was splashing away. Russell himself turned his handsome, solemn face towards me.

'Don't follow you.'

'If you want to see me, why don't you just come round on your own?'

A pause; and then the patient, puzzled voice: 'Still don't see your point, Vincent.'

Always an implacable sod, my big brother.)

He came by a little later than usual this time, about one-thirty. I was still up, and should have been marking essays. I tended to do that sort of thing at that sort of time, as if my professional duties were so loathsome to me that they could only be done at an hour usually reserved for the darkest of deeds, for murder and torture, rape . . . But what I was actually doing at that late hour was the same as I'd been doing for almost the whole evening: lounging upon my sofa, letting my mind grind over my troubles, and occasionally looking down at the little boy who lay beside me under an England World Cup '70 quilt. The child was deep in sleep; not even the hammering on my front door disturbed him.

When I opened the door – a few inches only at first, for the block I lived in had its share of undesirables, both resident and visiting – I found my tall brother outside, gazing down at me. 'Val's got a problem,' Russell announced. I opened the door wide. My brother came in, followed by two strangers, one of them a young woman. 'This is Val,' Russell told me. I looked at the girl appreciatively. She was about seventeen or eighteen, with a beautiful doll's face and a pair of the most perfect legs I had ever seen. They were on view practically from where they joined to where they disappeared into her low-rise white go-go boots. These last struck me as a little incongruous in fact; I hadn't seen any like them for a good few years, not on the King's Road at any rate, where the look was now all flowing, looning, hippie gear, buckskin fringes and yards of kohl. Her blonde hair too, I noted, seemed styled in a rather *passé* manner, heavily lacquered and built up in a version of the old beehive. Still in spite of it all, she was lovely.

Her full, coral-pink tinged lips parted now: 'I'd say hello,' she said, 'but I'm desperate.'

I opened the lavatory door for her. She dived inside. Closed the door behind her.

'And this is Goldy,' Russell said.

I looked at this second stranger with interest too. He was quite different from the usual rat-faced, dapper young men that Russell brought around. He wasn't young – about fifty-five, perhaps, even sixty. A little portly chap, almost completely bald, save for a patch of grizzled hair at the back, and extravagant sideburns of the same intricately curled grey. And he was dressed not in high South-east London fashion like the average of Russell's acquaintance, but soberly, richly. A honey-coloured shorty overcoat, cashmere I guessed, over a good dark suit, three-piece. Crisp white shirt and a tie of a subdued, formal design like that of a rather exclusive club. He looked infinitely respectable. And prosperous. Chairman of ICI? Consultant at a London teaching hospital? Senior academic? I knew he would be none of these really of course – but still, what was he doing in my brother's company?

His manner towards me too was quite different from the norm among Russell's friends. They usually came on very aggressive. Summed me up pretty fast as a bit of a mug, easy touch. Soft. Looking around with their sharp, assessing eyes at my two-and-a-half poky rooms, it would be: 'How much you pay for this, Vincent?' And when I told them, 'That's a fuckin' disgrace!' they'd cry out indignantly, as if it was *my* fault. And: 'Over in Brixton? Or Noo Cross? Vince, you wouldn't believe what I could get you for that kind of money.' Goldy, in contrast, seemed rather shy with me. A nod and a mumble when we were introduced, and then when – in deference to Val, for an unexpectedly robust cascade could now be heard through the toilet door – we three men moved into the living-room, he refused the offer of a drink, and darted off into a corner where he began to study my collection of paperbacks with great concentration.

Waiting for Val to rejoin us, my brother and I talked carefully together. Russell was looking well, I was glad to see, and prosperous. We spoke for a while of our then ailing parents. They were still running their newsagent's shop at the time and it was doubtful how much longer they could do this. But they'd had the business for thirty-five years (we boys had grown up over the shop), and they were both independent, proud people. Neither Russell nor I fancied being the one to tell them it was time to quit.

Having debated that knotty problem to no useful conclusion as usual, we gave it up and switched to talking about our respective wives. Russell's Anthea was taking her driving test tomorrow and was pretty nervous about it apparently (she passed). I had nothing even that interesting to tell about my own wife (my first wife, that is) who had removed herself and our little girl from the home we had shared not long ago and was now living in considerable contentment (according to her rare letters) and in much greater comfort (which wouldn't be hard) thousands of miles distant from me.

'Glad you kicked her out now, are you?' Russell asked.

It hadn't been like that at all, but I nodded my head anyway.

'That's right,' Russell said approvingly. 'She never fitted in over here, did she?'

Val came in then. Goldy turned to her with evident relief, and it seemed as if he wanted to leave right away. But she took the drink I held out to her. Goldy accepted the change of plan with good grace, shrugged his way out of his overcoat. The two of them settled down upon the sofa, next to the baby boy who slept on all unaware. 'This yours?' Val asked, turning her cornflower-blue eyes upon me. I told her he wasn't, that he belonged to the couple upstairs who were out at a party tonight. She gazed down at the child for a moment, then gave a dainty little shudder. 'I hate the thought of havin' one,' she said. 'Till I'm lots older anyway. I've been so relieved since Goldy had the IUD put in.'

Goldy dimpled with self-conscious pride, as if he had performed the operation himself, and his pudgy fingers sought out and squeezed the nearest of the girl's gorgeous thighs.

She clearly had a remarkable effect on him. His shyness had dropped quite away. Now he looked around him boldly. In my little flat the living-room doubled as a study. The table was littered with the signs of my professional existence – books, typewriter, stacks of A4 paper (and many screwed-up sheets of the same), a pile of student essays, half of them still waiting to be marked. Goldy looked at all this

academic clutter with evident approval. And then transferred his complacent gaze back to me.

'So this is Russell's clever little bruvver.'

Immediately I breathed easier. I knew my man now; no
mystery here. That accent. Those whingeing vowels. I could
place him within a mile or two. Not as far south as my own
native Penge (or the more up-scale Beckenham where my
parents, against the evidence, always insisted on locating our
family home). But below Greenwich, say, or Battersea. The
clothes might be Jermyn Street. The accent was pure
Burton's and the Fifty Shilling Tailors. It was Lewisham,
Brockley, Catford. Somewhere round there.

And in his turn Goldy thought he knew me. Russell's
clever little brother. I ducked my head modestly. It was so.
Couldn't be avoided.

'Show 'em your article, Vincent,' Russell commanded. 'I
told him about it.'

Obediently I recovered the learned journal from the
bookcase and handed it over to Goldy. It fell easily open
at my contribution.

'Actually it's more of a Note than an article,' I muttered
self-consciously.

Goldy didn't seem to pay much attention to that, though it
was true enough. Two-and-a-half pages long. Representing,
I did not fail to remind myself yet again, eight long years on
the frontiers of scholarship. Eight-and-a-half by now.

But that, I knew, was just an author's bitter thoughts.
Goldy seemed delighted by my creation. He slipped on a
pair of steel-rimmed bi-focals and held the journal out
before him.

' "Some Laundry Accounts from the Household of Lord Shelburne," ' he read out in measured tones. ' "1776 to 1778".' He beamed benevolently at the title page and then turned overleaf to where I had signed off. ' "Vincent Stabler".' He looked up. 'A Cambridge man?'

'Well – at the time.'

He took off his glasses and glanced at my brother.

'You must be very proud, Russell,' he said.

Russell nodded soberly. Goldy passed the journal to Val, who blinked down at it incuriously, and then he said to me, 'Where are you working now, son?'

I told him, and his face brightened. He named one of the college's board of trustees and asked if I knew him. I told him I didn't know the man to talk to, but of course by reputation. Everybody knew him by reputation. He was a then-prominent Labour politician, who had been recently discarded from serious affairs and kicked upstairs. As well as a title, the Party had arranged for his premature and reluctant retirement from serious politics to be sweetened with several company directorships and a more or less honorary post at the university college where I worked. This was not at all to the satisfaction of most of the junior members of the college, staff and students. Left-wing puritans almost to a man and woman, they viewed the statesman as a particularly ripe specimen of social democratic compromise with the Enemy, and his erratic career as reeking with tomfoolery, drunkenness, and general straying from the shining path of socialism. I could not imagine why we were talking about him now.

'I know him quite well,' Goldy said.

I felt, and knew I must have looked, most disbelieving. 'I'm in his book,' Goldy insisted. (The statesman had recently published his memoirs.) 'You look in the back. Under Stern. Eric Stern. That's me.' Still I was clearly not convinced. Goldy's mouth turned downwards in disappointment, and a certain pall hung over the rest of his visit that night, which saddened me a bit for I'd found I had an instinctive liking for this roly-poly little man. Nevertheless, when he and Val got up to go at last, he seemed to forgive my rudeness in doubting his word, and offered to put a word 'in the right ear' for me at the university.

'I like to help bright young men,' he said.

I shuddered and begged him not to. My situation was currently so difficult at work that to receive the endorsement of such an equivocal figure as I guessed Goldy to be might have finished me off, I thought. Goldy again looked hurt, and in fact his gaze took on a rather dangerous aspect. So I quickly thanked him profusely for his offer, arguing at the same time that it would hardly be fair on all the other poor lecturers to take such an advantage.

Goldy relaxed, seemed to acknowledge my arguments, but was not convinced by them. 'Ah, he's still wet behind 'em, eh, Russ?' he said. 'Don't know how to work his contacts, does he? It's not what you know, son,' he murmured with the air of someone divulging a formula of almost masonic obscurity, 'it's who.'

'That's right, boss,' Russell said impassively, helping Goldy into his gorgeous overcoat.

'Still,' said Goldy, 'I'm obliged to him for helping out my little girl . . . Show our appreciation, Russell.'

He led Val out of the living-room. Russell, giving me an amused glance, opened his wallet and then laid three five-pound notes on top of my typewriter. I started to protest (not all that hard: fifteen pounds represented a good slice of my monthly take-home pay), but my brother cut me off. 'Take it,' he ordered. 'He's feeling good tonight. He won eight hundred quid at the club.'

At the open front door I thanked Goldy for the present a little awkwardly.

'It's nothing,' he said grandly. 'I know you university fellers can always do with a bit extra.' Then he dropped back a pace to regard Russell and me standing together under the corridor light. 'I like that,' he said. 'Brains and—' He stepped forward and lightly punched Russell's upper arm, laughed up into his sombre face. 'Brawn! Good combination.' He gathered Val to him, waved – 'Then I'll be seeing you, Vincent, eh?' – and set off again into the dark.

The next day I stopped in at Dillons and looked up a copy of the memoirs of the eminent politician Goldy had claimed as a friend. *Nothing If Not a Crusade* it was called. Sure enough I found a 'Stern, Eric' in the index. I turned to the indicated page. The paragraph ran as follows:

Eric 'Goldy' Stern and I have been pals ever since the days, towards the end of the War, when I was taking my first tentative steps in local politics and he in the construction industry of which he has been such a luminary ever since. It has been a mutually profitable association, rich in comradeship and shared laughter. Rich in shared achievement too. Its true monuments lie in those imposing tower blocks that march like giants – twenty and thirty storeys high – across the length and breadth of London's great south-of-the-river. In these days the trendy moaners and doom-sayers of the Press and the universities have succeeded in blackening the reputation of buildings of this type, calling them inhumane, hideous and – since the unfortunate collapse of one of the blocks on the Ronan Point Estate in Canning Town, together with the attendant fatalities – even dangerous. All I will say is that such complaints were never heard in the early days from the decent simple folk who were able to escape from the old disgraceful Victorian slums into those 'towers of progress' (as I called them in a speech at the Town Hall, Battersea in 1959), that such men as Goldy Stern have spent their careers – and, literally, their blood, sweat and tears – providing for them.

II

To my surprise, over the next year or so I became quite friendly with Eric 'Goldy' Stern. He took me out to eat several times – never alone, Russell and Val always came along, and usually one or two other of Goldy's employees. (The rat-faced young men, I was pleased to find, were much less aggressive towards me now they saw I was on good terms with the boss.) Other times, with just Val and Russell in tow, he came over to my flat to pass an evening. (As I write this it seems we were hardly ever out of each other's company, but I suppose if I counted them up these meetings would total around a dozen over the eighteen months I knew him.) And we would talk. Or rather Goldy would talk, sometimes into the small hours, the subject almost always being himself. His early life and blood-drenched times. Understandably, because they had heard all Goldy's stories before, and had if anything a surfeit of his presence in their daily lives, the other two responded with much less enthusiasm to these tales than I did. At some point in the evening Val was bound to become tired and crotchety. And Goldy, with a fatherly smile for both of them, would order Russell to take her home in the Bentley. Then alone at last, sipping expensive brandy (after his first exposure to my drinks cabinet, Goldy brought over his own supply next time), we two would plunge straight back into a fierce and murky wonderland.

'Did I ever tell you, Vincent, about the time . . .'

It was a treat for him to dazzle Russell's clever little brother. And I *was* dazzled. Extortion, blackmail, beatings, bloody days and nights of revenge: they blazed around my head like TV newsreel of the day's fighting in some cruel faraway war. Afterwards, it is true, I was able to work out a more sober estimate of what I was being told. Patterns began to take shape. To hear Goldy talk he was, as he sat there – the plump smiling figure in the Jermyn Street suit – in the very midst of the criminal saturnalia he was describing. But I began to notice two things about his stories. First, that when I pressed him for more details it almost always seemed to emerge that it wasn't exactly *him* who had been the actual perpetrator of each ghastly deed. Not his hand that had wielded the cosh, nor his finger that pulled the trigger. Nor – remembering one especially gory narrative –

his teeth that had fastened on a rival's nose and torn it practically off its hinge. No, that was always the work of a mate, a crony, a sidekick. Or, increasingly, an employee. Some other fellow anyway, not him at all. And I certainly don't believe that Goldy was trying here to disguise his own responsibility. It was the other way round. The truth came out reluctantly; he would much rather have shone before me as the desperate, merciless character he'd passed himself off as before my questioning wore him down.

The other thing I noticed was that there was a very specific time zone in which all the dark deeds he'd been involved in had happened. He hardly ever spoke of the 1960s, for instance, that recently departed decade which had been so rich in gangster-heroes, most of whom by now were either in jail or dead: the Krays, and Jack the Hat, the 'Axeman' Frank Mitchell and, in Goldy's own neck of the woods, the Richardson brothers and 'Mad Frankie' Fraser. Goldy emphatically was not of this breed, and indeed I got the clear impression that, if he hadn't exactly gone into hiding while these dangerous and unstable characters were flourishing, he had prudently opted for a much lower profile during that time. For him they had been years of consolidation and quiet expansion, a period when, in particular, he had been developing his contacts among the borough councils and local Labour parties that fell in his bailiwick. He was a great contributor to the latter, and not just, I'm convinced, or even mainly for cynical business reasons. The Labour Party of that time, of Hugh Gaitskell and Harold Wilson, with its easygoing welfare socialism and unemphatic Zionism, suited Goldy fine. He was genuinely glad to know that ordinary folk were doing so much better than when he was a young man. I remember him speaking of a friend of his from long ago, raised in the same mean streets, taught at the same threadbare disgrace for a school, like him shoved out into the world in his early teens to earn a living. All of this man's children had gone to university, and Goldy was genuinely moved by the fact: 'Could never have happened, Vincent, never even been dreamed of when I was young. Those were terrible times, I'm telling you.'

I had no reason to doubt him. But couldn't help noticing that it was to those times that he mainly took us when we talked. However bleak and hopeless the background, it was evident that for him these were the years that contained most of the glamour and adventure of his life. Back in the late Thirties when he was getting his start in the scrap metal trade in New Cross and Lewisham. Or at the end of the War and in the years just after when he was muscling his way into the construction industry on one or other of the many rebuilding projects that were in progress then along the South Bank. Dates like 1938 or 1947, or at the latest the early Fifties – these had been the glory years of Goldy's career, when he, or at least his associates, had fought with tooth, nail, and whatever else was handy to win a place in the sun. And I came to see that for once it was I who was being given a lesson in history; and the special charm of these occasions for Goldy, I knew, was that they gave him a chance to bring forward his youth again, and to show off his roaring days for my professional appreciation.

Sometimes in this period when I met with my brother, just the two of us, Russell would deride me for my sentimental, spectatorish view of his boss. And it is true that I was able to listen to these tales of brutality, corruption, extortion, even – Goldy's voice always dropped down a note or two when he came to this – of murder with no more feeling for the pain they represented than if I had been watching a James Cagney or an Edward G. Robinson film. And that is how they really were for me, and my only excuse for my blindness. He was a great storyteller, a spellbinder. Like some giant of *film noir*, threading his simple melodramas through complex and claustrophobic foregrounds of fear and darkness, so that I seemed to see before me the swirling pre-war fogs, the dank cobbled alleys, grim-faced young men cradling sawn-off shotguns. The South London pigeon-chests swathed in voluminous wide-striped suits. Black shirts. Silver ties. Peaked caps or slouched trilbies. The flash of a razor under a dim streetlamp. Running footsteps fading into the murk. A hoarse prayer whispered against a shining, rain-soaked pavement. Mother of Mercy, is this the end of – well, fill in the name of any one of at least half-a-dozen victims that Goldy, with the modest but justified pride of an opening bat after a big hundred, laid claim to over the nights when he was a guest in my rooms.

I so loved to have him there, for his solid successful presence almost as much as his stories. I found they pushed away for a while the sorrowful confusion that, since my wife and daughter's departure, always seemed about to engulf me.

Three

I

'Many years ago' (he began), 'nearly twenty in fact, long before all of you were born, politics in this country were in a bit of a turmoil.' (*Turmoil*? Would Bubbles have used that word? He couldn't remember. Probably not.) 'Things weren't looking too good,' he explained. 'The new Conservative government was in serious trouble, and its prime minister already deeply unpopular. Can anyone tell me who that prime minister was?'

In the assembly hall, the ranks of eyes stared back at him. The silence was stony. Sixty or seventy faces – he was taking two classes at once; it was normal, the schools liked to get their money's worth – black, white, brown faces, each of which seemed to be showing the same expression of blank incuriosity. Again it was nothing out of the ordinary. Bubbles had liked to pose the same question early on, and was not too worried if she didn't get a correct, or any answer. She found it a useful tool all the same.

'Lets me know how much they know. Then I can work out at what level I can talk to them.'

Thing was, Vincent always wondered, how could she be sure that the refusal to answer was out of ignorance or just plain bloody-mindedness? Listening to her put this and other questions to studiedly silent young audiences just like this one, the scale of ignorance that was exposed had seemed sometimes incredible. She had drawn a blank at such posers as: what is Parliament? where is Parliament? what is democracy? what is a general election? who is the current prime minister? name the capital of your country. Nothing. Zero. Zilch. How could they be so clueless?

'It was Margaret Thatcher,' he said at last. Somebody in one of the first few rows farted loudly. For a moment he wondered if it was intended as a sort of rough political sally. But that hope died as he looked out again on his audience. The name that had dominated absolutely the public life of Britain for a dozen years rang no bells in this room. Nobody here was at home for Mrs T. Serve her right, he thought. 'Lo, like Nineveh and Tyre . . .' And so on. He had never liked the woman, detecting in her, even while she was in opposition, long before her later war-flecked beatification, an unhealthy level of messianic self-importance.

Actually, he remembered now, that had been Bubbles' perception mainly, having of course many more opportunities of viewing her: the tearoom, the lobbies, the Chamber itself. Himself, he had only set eyes on her twice in the flesh. Once, in late '82, standing talking to a group of respectful journalists in the Strangers' Bar; and earlier, also in the House, when she had appeared groping myopically along the dim and remote corridor in which Bubbles, as a brand-new MP, had been allotted a workplace. There was a desk there, a seat, possibly a phone, he couldn't remember now. He did remember the cobwebs and the general grime, the solitude. He worked there most days of the week and it was rare to be interrupted by another human being, and then usually only by a hurrying secretary or researcher. Once he had seen the Clerk of the House who was a very important person, of course. Still nothing had prepared him for a visitation from the actual Leader of HM's Opposition, as she then was. Mrs Thatcher appeared lost and not to be pleased about it.

'Can I get through to the Members' lobby along here?' she asked.

Vincent had been unable to help her, having not yet committed to memory even that part of the building to which his researcher's pass gave him access. She had cast on him a single impatient glance, and then had proceeded on her way. Clearly she must have eventually found the path back to civilisation for he read in the paper on the way home that she had been in fine form at Question Time that afternoon, teasing the prime minister over his economic policy.

II

'The Labour Party—' And should he really have to identify that organisation for this bunch of dimwits? No! there were limits after all. '– was in great disarray. The failure of the Callaghan government—' Sod 'em, they'd just have to pick it up as he went along: '. . . defeat at the general election of '79 . . . widespread demoralisation . . . particularly the centre and right of the parliamentary Party . . . implicated in the disasters of the past . . . Harold Wilson . . . on the other hand the Left now saw its opportunity . . . deselection

of moderate members . . . extremist conference resolutions
. . . Tony Benn . . . Michael Foot . . .'

He had lost them all by now. To the original indifference
of their expressions had been added a glaze of irritated
bafflement. Some had begun to talk among themselves.
Fairly quietly so far, but the rustle of crisp packets was
continuous. He wondered what lies had been told to en-
courage them to go quietly into the assembly hall in the first
place. Were they expecting him to show slides? Run
movies? Play records? He had none. He had nothing. Only
his memories. And a blow-by-blow familiarity with the
great events of the 1980s.

Yet with no more than those, Bubbles had been able to
hold such audiences if not spellbound, then moderately
interested at least. And it was not just schoolkids. A
surprising number of interested groups – colleges, WIs,
local history societies, hospices, Darby & Joans – wanted to
hear from her. In fact most of their income in the last few
years had come from those lectures. He had found something to do, three mornings a week, in a picture library in
Streatham, filing and helping organise the catalogue. But
that wouldn't have kept their ship afloat. It was she who did
that. Fees from occasional articles or reviews. Or obituaries.
And most of all the lecturing. If he could only remember
how she had done it. He ought to be able to. He had
accompanied her to many of her lectures, say one in five at
least. And more and more as her disease tightened its hold.
To see her on to the bus or the train, to help her on and off
the platform, to make sure there was a chair there if she
needed it, and water, and her pills.

What words? What gestures, flourishes, jokes had she used to put the story over – and why couldn't he remember them? How had she *said* it? For certain it was not like a particularly pompous editorial writer in the *Daily Telegraph* circa 1955 which was all he seemed able to manage.

(But then why should he do any better? He had told Farquarson at the agency that he was not his wife, had never been a public figure, had not one-tenth of her skills as a communicator. Farquarson said he understood, but would be terribly grateful if Vincent could just fulfil the last engagement she'd accepted. So as not to let the customer down he said he would, but that would be all. Finito. Farquarson said he'd get back to him on that.)

'In these difficult circumstances, three prominent members of Labour's centre and right – Shirley Williams, Bill Rodgers and David Owen – supported by a number of their parliamentary friends and followers, began to consider together whether they should leave their old party and form a new one dedicated to the kind of democratic left-of-centre politics they all believed in. They were soon joined in their discussions by another leading figure of Labour's immediate past: ex-Chancellor of the Exchequer Roy Jenkins, who had just completed a stint with the European Commission in Brussels, and was looking for a way back into British politics. In this way the original Gang of Three became the still more famous Gang of Four . . .'

He paused again, took a sip from the glass of water that had been placed at his right hand before the lecture started. He noted that the level of conversation had risen somewhat, but the noise was still not yet overpowering. Discouragingly though, the talkers included the two teachers who'd been sent along to supervise. They were nattering away at each other, sublimely indifferent to the lecturer's attempts to interest them. It was most irritating. If he'd had any chalk to hand, he thought he might have flung it at their heads.

'The result of all these deliberations,' he raised his voice to report, 'was that a new party, called the Social Democratic Party – SDP for short – was launched in March 1981, committing itself to an electoral alliance with the Liberals. By then fourteen MPs – thirteen Labour, and one Conservative – had already resigned their party whips and were part of the SDP's founding presence in Parliament. One more Labour MP came over in July, another in September, seven more after the Labour Party conference in October, and two more in November . . .'

November '81 was when *they* had got out. It had seemed exactly the right time to go. If anything they feared they had left it too late. In the opinion polls the SDP–Liberal Alliance had moved decisively ahead of Labour in August, and of both other parties in October. And results on the ground were showing that these were not just pollsters' fantasies. At Warrington in July, Roy Jenkins had done amazingly well in almost capturing one of the safest Labour seats in the country. Now up in Lancashire Shirley Williams was poised to take the Crosby seat. The crowds that turned out to support her were tumultuous, triumphant. The bandwagon was rolling unstoppably. If the Stablers waited any longer they might miss it altogether. At the least they would always carry a johnny-come-lately stigma. If the polls and the evidence of the by-elections were to be believed, the Alliance stood a good chance of forming the next government. The jobs were already being divvied up, and there was every sign that the rule of first-come first-served would be rigorously applied.

'This of course was a most exciting time for those involved. A sense of freshness, of newness in the air, like spring. Almost like revolution. "Breaking the mould" we called it . . .' The stale old mould of British politics and national life. To set out on uncharted seas; with a band of trusted like-minded companions; ah yes! 'Truly—' Vincent allowed himself a nostalgic smile. ' "Bliss was it that dawn to be alive/But to be young—" '

The words froze on his lips as he looked up to see the awful apathy of genuine youth before him. But then why *should* they care? Here they were, late 1998 – twenty bloody years ago all this stuff he was gabbing on about had happened . . . And yet – if only he could explain it to them. Explain how *thrilling* it had been. How inspiring! But even she had never been able to convey that to her audiences, not altogether. For beyond all their calculations about what would be best for her career, besides the relief they craved at being able to get away at last from the endless bitter squabbles with the Leftists in the constituency, they were drawn to their decision too by simpler, purer motives. Hope. Loyalty to something above mere Party. A willingness to join a crusade that they believed sincerely would do good for their country, and a readiness to sacrifice whatever they must to see it succeed. But how to convey all that in mere words?

And the truth was it was so hard to disentangle the

threads. What had been most important in persuading them to sign up to the SDP? The patriotism or the calculation? The stroking or the heart-searching? Was it the flattering invitations – morning coffee at Shirley's modest flat in Rochester Row, or lunch at Roy and Jennifer's spacious retreat in East Hendred 'so we can have a little chat before you make up your minds'? Or the cosy dinner at L'Amico with Bill and Ian for a 'purely hypothetical' discussion of what Bubbles thought she could contribute to the new Party; a famous comedian, sympathetic to the Cause, dropping by towards the end of the meal for a friendly exchange of insults? (How it had all contrasted with the dreary anonymity that was Bubbles' lot as one of a couple of hundred other Labour backbenchers, where it was a red-letter day to be awarded a distant nod in passing from the most junior of ministers.) Or was it the long nights at home when the two of them had almost prayerfully gone over and over the reasons for and against leaving? Or the intense, sometimes tearful discussions with the few members left in their constituency Party they still felt close to? Some of them had been horrified to think they were planning to go. Even more were ready to jump ship too. Equal passion on either side.

Still they couldn't make up their minds. August turned into September. October brought the Party conference. Brighton. The atmosphere was sulphurous. The Stablers were regarded with intense suspicion. On the seafront an MP from a Merseyside constituency had rounded on them to shout 'Why don't you just *fuck off*?' Inside the hall, conference repeatedly passed motions that were almost crazy in their detachment from reality. All the while from the platform Michael Foot, presiding over his first conference as Leader, smiled blandly down on the disaster, blinking through his thick spectacles like a bewildered old owl.

And so a few weeks later they did just fuck off. In the Commons Bubbles took her seat on the SDP benches. Vincent had watched her proudly from the Strangers' Gallery. Through all the hoots from the Labour side and the brave cheers from the little group of Alliance MPs, she kept her composure. She smiled up at him. He waved back at her. He had no doubt at all that she – that *they* – were doing the right thing, the only thing. And how could either of them have suspected that a little group of islands in the South Atlantic was shortly to render all their calculations, hopes and prospects entirely barren? As well as those of thousands of others, of course.

'The invasion of the Falklands by Argentina in the spring of 1982,' he carried on now, 'and even more Mrs Thatcher's vigorous resistance to it, changed the face of British politics utterly and in a direction that was not at all helpful to the prospects of our new Party—'

A hand suddenly waved energetically before him. A question? A miracle. He pointed to the waving boy. Sitting in the third row. Slender. Pale. Red Hair. Looked not unintelligent, at least in present company. Vincent felt his hopes rise.

'Yes?'

'Yeah, right,' the boy was smirking. 'Did you know you got hair growing out of your nose?'

Uproar. Great hilarity all round. The teachers were on

their feet, calling out wearily: 'All right, Jason, that'll do . . .'
Jason meanwhile was receiving from his peers the honours
due to such a mordant stroke. High-fives and happy
whoops. Vincent waited for order to be restored. He was
not that put out. There was usually a Jason on these
occasions. Or a Darren, or a Ryan, or a Tracey, or a Stacey.
His wife had faced such nuisances often, and even she had
never really found a good method of dealing with them.
Certainly exchanging insults was no help. That way disaster
lay. And it was prehistoric to think of hitting the little
buggers any more – which was a good thing, for most of
them looked as if they could hit back a lot harder. In fact all
one could actually do was wait out the shit-storm, step over
the resultant mess, and then move on regardless. It was like
politics really.

Four

I

Looking back on those sessions with Goldy Stern, I know that a part of my growing affection for the man derived from pleasure in seeing the good care he was taking of my brother. My feelings for Russell had been hag-ridden with guilt for so long, and it was a relief to see him bloom into prosperity under Goldy's guiding hand. The problem had been that in our family mythology I, the younger brother, was the success and he the failure. This myth was so strong and so carefully nurtured and encouraged in every possible way by our doting parents, that even the fact that I knew it to be increasingly untrue and that, I'm sure, Russell half-suspected the same, didn't stop both of us deep down believing in it.

Its origins were quite simple and once commonplace. One day at the age of eleven years and two months, Russell went to take an exam at school. He had a stomach upset during it; the family myth held that it was the kipper he had eaten for breakfast. He asked to leave the room, but was persuaded to stay on as the exam was so important for his future. As indeed it was. He failed it, and the following September set off for his first day at the secondary modern school round the corner to join all the other failures. Three years later I passed the same exam and consequently was admitted to a prestigious semi-public school (founded 1833), some five miles up the railway line towards

London. This is how I became a success, Russell a failure.

This myth though had so many ramifications. Some things were partly true about it, the rest false. We – my parents, me – used to always charitably think of Russell as the 'victim' of an unfair system. As he was, of course, and the circumstance so often rehearsed among us, at times depressed him deeply. But on the other hand, the victim grew up, term by term, a fairly well-integrated and optimistic young man. Whatever was wrong with his school – the drab and poorly maintained buildings, the brutal fights in the playground, the low standard of teaching – was at least wrong in an uncomplicated way. I, in my loftier surroundings . . . well, things were not so clear for me. The curious mixture of post-Second World War socialist idealism and Edwardian public school rigmarole that my school promoted was almost guaranteed to turn out a generation of schizophrenics. We were urged to consider ourselves as in the very vanguard of the new (pink-tinged) British dawn. At the same time we were being beaten diligently and regularly upon our buttocks for, say, wearing the middle buttons of our uniform jackets done up, or for not knowing in a 'Colours test' that R.E.F. Barraclough (Tennyson's) had scored 131 not out against Merchant Taylor's in 1924, and that H.T. O'Mara (Dickens') had been hanged in '46 as a German spy.

II

I could go on – and on. Suffice to say that at the end of his school days, Russell, with the clarity of mind his knockabout but straightforward education had given him, deliberated carefully and exhaustively about his future. One of his close friends joined the police. Another emigrated to Canada. A third, with the help of family connections, got a start in crime. Russell finally chose the last route, arranging to be taken on at a certain garage in Bellingham, getting a thorough initial grounding in the art of 'ringing' stolen luxury cars for the export trade, before moving on to the intricate and demanding tasks of actually stealing them to order and then delivering them to the customer. And all these years since, however much harassed and pursued by our well-meaning parents' cries of 'Poor old Russell' and 'Why not talk it over with Vincent?', he had been patiently, tirelessly building up his career.

While Russell was thus sensibly carving out a warm place for himself in a cold world, I, the success, basking in my parents' admiration, took the path of formal achievement. Exams were passed, universities attended, a doctoral thesis almost written, elderly and middle-aged dons buttered-up, and finally a lecturing job landed – pretty nearly all for just the pleasure of hearing those old task-masters' applause. And Russell's. For he too joined willingly in the feeding of my vanity, many times listening in humble silence to my glib opinions and fat-headed pronouncements on every subject under the sun. He even listened, without throwing a punch at my head, to the preposterous career advice which (at my parents' urging and to my own great pleasure) I was always offering him, only once in a while murmuring a gentle 'Well, I'm a bit old for O-levels now, aren't I?' I even offered to coach him!

All I can say in my favour is that part of my motive in patronising Russell this way was that I felt deeply sometimes the shame of our mythic selves. Deep down – before even I came to see them as all lures and traps – I wanted *him* to have passed the bloody exams. I wanted myself, the younger, to come to *him* for advice . . . I believe I wanted this.

And yet it seemed to give me little pleasure to find, as the Sixties wore on, that in some measure my wishes were on the way to coming to pass. Even before Russell's rise to power in Goldy's organisation, the old myth was fragmenting – but I was not cheering about it much. Our differing fortunes in marriage helped a long way in this process. Russell teamed up with a cheerful, pretty, home-loving and -making girl (known naturally around my parents' house as 'poor old Anthea'). I got something quite different, discovering her during my postgraduate year at Berkeley, California, and bringing her home in the autumn, an exotic and increasingly frantic transplant, first to Cambridge, and then to share my flat, friends, life in the then-grim surrounds of Fulham Road and Bloomsbury.

True to say that I could not at the time imagine taking Anthea for wife as a gift. She seemed to have three subjects of conversation only – Russell, their children, and their new 'purpose-built' house in Brockley. My own wife, Matty MacBride (a name which hardly suggested her actual ancestral mix of Polish and Italian with, so she claimed, just a splash of Cherokee), used to refer to Anthea invariably as 'that dumb *hausfrau*', and I could see her point. Nevertheless it was also true, though at the time increasingly unfashionable to mention, that Russell got a peaceful life from her, plus a nice clean home, breakfast in bed every day, and a hot dinner whenever he chose to come home for it – and I got driven nearly crazy. Again it's a fact that I wouldn't have wanted much to have Russell's two noisy, healthy, grubby boys growing up around me. But then too it wasn't so good to have a little daughter – however sweet and clever and loving – who was now growing up so far away, apparently so traumatised by her brief stay in my household that she couldn't be allowed to speak on the phone to me, couldn't write, couldn't – perish the thought – ever possibly visit her dad.

(Oh the pain of it, the fucking horrible pain.

'Why didn't you stop her going?' Russell asked me once. 'At least from taking the kid with her?'

'What would you have done?' I asked helplessly. It was quite frightening then to hear what Russell would have done.)

Another thing that was chipping away all the time at our myth was that my earnest and repetitious advice about his career began to look ever more fatuous as mine started to falter and fail. It was not possible to keep this a secret. There is such a great gap between a snotty young graduate with his brand-new first-class degree and confident ambitions and a twenty-nine-year-old junior lecturer with one article published and no promotions behind him (and none in prospect either). The fact was I had grown horribly bored with the scholarly life (entirely my own fault of course, for I had gone into it for quite other rewards than for its own sake); and bored and disgusted too by the displays of mediocrity (particularly my own), careerism, politicking, backbiting, mendacity, and prejudice that I had found in that world. This state of mind bred in its turn a lethargy and a lack of interest in my professional duties which had already brought me to a difficult conference with my departmental chief. It happened the day after Goldy's sixtieth birthday party. A huge affair, no expense spared, it was held at 'Heath's Edge', the battlemented castle (built in 1925) that Goldy called home, situated on one of the leafy roads that led up to Blackheath from behind Chiesemans department store in Lewisham. I had come straight up from there to my college in the early morning light and was now in the senior common room, trying to snooze before my first tutorial. The head of department sat down opposite. He looked at me in my stained, dishevelled party gear, and then asked politely: 'Are you happy here, Vincent?'

'Yes,' I lied.

He nodded. Thought for a long moment. And then, still most politely: 'Why?'

He entered then on a monologue concerning people who had left the academic life and found much happiness and prosperity outside it. He suggested delicately that he envied me my freedom. I was young. Not yet committed. There were so many choices open to me.

'Avoid the treadmill if you possibly can, Vincent,' he advised me. 'Get out while you're still young.'

'But I don't see it as a treadmill,' I fibbed heatedly. 'I don't want to get out.'

'No?' he said, sounding very disappointed. 'You don't?'

The whole thing left me shaken to the core and feeling – I was sure appropriately – that if I did not jump from my job, in a very short while I would certainly be pushed. And while our parents remained happily oblivious to my problems, Russell was more observant. And indeed, feeling his comprehension, I did open up to him a couple of times, and tried to hint at my disappointments. I don't think he entirely believed the measure of my desperation, or how much trouble I was in. Nor – because of that part of our myth which required him always to be proud of me – that he particularly wanted to believe. But he could see that, for whatever reason, my life seemed to me barren and sad, and so that I too was in train to becoming a failure. Real failure this time, not the phantom version we had wished on him, which had concealed an authentic success. And surely, in some corner of his soul, he must have wanted this. As the older brother, he must have done.

Five

I

Lunch: a ham and cucumber sandwich from the petrol-station (£2.90). He ate it at home, in the kitchen, listening to the end of *The World At One*. He'd been invited to stay for school dinner, but had declined with little pretence of regret and to the evident relief of his hosts. It had been a sorry sort of occasion altogether – a 'no-no' as Bubbles had used to categorise similar fiascos. Which she'd rarely had to face. Her style and sense of humour and courage had carried her through against the trickiest of audiences.

After lunch he decided to go up to the bedroom for a nap. The phone rang just as his foot hit the top stair. Wearily he retraced his steps to the living-room. It was Farquarson at the agency. Vincent fell immediately on the defensive, but before he could get out his repertoire of excuses for the recent performance, he heard from the other end of the line:

'Congratulations!'

For what? Vincent thought at first he had said that aloud. In fact, he realised then, he'd not uttered a word. He was still standing there, gripping the phone, waiting for Farquarson to declare himself. If it was a joke, a sarcastic comment on his ineptitude, he could do without it. It had already been a long day, and it was only just half over.

'Hello?' said Farquarson.

'Yes. I'm here. What do you mean "congratulations"?'

'On your storming performance this morning. The school's been on the phone just now. Terribly pleased with how it went. The kids—'

'They hated me. So did the teachers. I was awful.'

He heard Farquarson breathing down the line. He seemed to be waiting for Vincent to finish his nonsense. In fact Vincent had done just that. He too now waited in silence.

'You must consider, Mr Stabler,' Farquarson began again in a voice calculated to soothe the most hysterical of clients, the angriest of customers, 'that you may not be an objective judge of your own performance—'

'And you should consider that I spent a lot of time watching my wife lecture and that I know the difference between a successful talk – what did you call it? "A storming performance" – and the kind of disaster that went on this morning.'

'Mrs Stabler – *Bubbles* – was a phenomenon. A force of nature. The most gifted of all my clients. Why she never became a star on radio or TV remains a mystery . . . You mustn't try and compare yourself with her.' And when Vincent tried to brush aside this attempt to soften today's humiliation: 'All I can say is, the school wants you back.'

'That school? Wants me? Back there?'

'In two weeks' time. If your calendar permits. To talk to their fourth-years. The same talk, they were clear about that. Oh, and I have a couple of other requests for you: Townswomen's Guild at Orpington on the nineteenth and the East Hove Horticultural Society on the twenty-fifth. First-class rail expenses goes with that one by the way. There and back.'

'Why on earth would a horticultural—'

'Who knows? Perhaps they get sick of talking about plants. Can I pencil you in?'

'No! It's absurd. I'm not an ex-MP. What on earth will they announce me as?'

'Husband of? Expert on? It's up to them. As long as you keep to your subject . . . You must realise, Mr Stabler, there's a great deal of interest in that.'

'In the SDP? I doubt it. Why should there be?'

'Nostalgia? Heritage? Part of our island story? Who knows? I can only say that when I suggest the topic there is always a very positive reaction. Would you be interested, by the way, in a cruise ship to the Baltic next July?'

'I tell you I was *terrible* at that bloody school—'

'Was there a riot? Did anyone hit you? Did anybody get hurt?'

'I suppose not.'

'Well, there you are. A triumph.'

II

In the end Farquarson rang off having persuaded Vincent to revisit the school in two weeks' time and at least to consider the Townswomen's Guild. Also they were now on first-name terms. It was Vincent and Terence now. Just as it had been Terence and Bubbles. For fifteen years, since that day, just a couple of weeks after the constituency had thrown them out, when Farquarson had rung to ask if she was interested in doing a couple of talks at a nearby College of Further Education? He'd been let down by a client, another former MP, who'd given him her name. The fee was £50 a visit then, minus Terence's 20 per cent. Bubbles took it. They felt they couldn't afford not to. There were not many visible signs of a future income just then. Bubbles would get a few months more of her parliamentary salary as severance pay. And she had negotiated a pretty good fee to write an article for the *Mail on Sunday* on what it felt like to be a brand-new ex-MP ('Fucking horrible,' had been Vincent's contribution when she asked him for ideas). That was it, and matters changed hardly at all in the next few months. They half-hoped for an approach from some big firm keen to use Bubbles' talents and experience in their boardroom. Many of her late colleagues, also chopped down at the poll, had slipped nimbly into directorships and executive posts. True they were likely to be ex-ministers, or had been otherwise prominent in their political lives, whereas Bubbles, frankly, had made few waves in Parliament or in the Party (either Party), except during the few startling days of her defection from the first of them.

(The tabloids had buzzed around her like bees round honey. Front page news for a couple of days. In the *Sun* a picture of her – above the caption 'Now the SDP Gets Sexy!!!' – sitting on her desk in the study of their house on Tressilian Road in the constituency, her skirt pulled up to her thigh, shapely legs on full display. She had wondered about doing that one. Feared it might hurt her parliamentary profile. First we need a profile, Vincent had assured her, then we can worry about hurting it. He was prone to that sort of judgement then. Quick, clever, unanswerable. What an ass. The photo had done her a lot of harm within her new Party, and elsewhere. Women's groups had denounced her as a traitor and gender-collaborator. Such things were taken very seriously then.)

In any case, apparently no commercial outfit was in need of honest competence and a good heart, which is what Bubbles had to offer when her days of worrying about a parliamentary profile were over. Nor, it turned out, was any charity, consumer association, educational establishment, or quango. In the end, Farquarson was their only hope.

Tossed out on the rubbish heap after all those years. Well, tough titty, yes, all right, but still . . . all that work, all those constituents dealt with and all their problems. The council flats that became available as if by magic. The teams of workers who arrived in a tower block to take care of damp problems that had been making the residents miserable for a dozen years. The mountains of rubbish that had been made to disappear. The paving stones that were replaced. The pensions that were paid, the electricity bills adjusted downwards, the lost child/husband/mother found. All because of a little pressure in the right places exerted by Bubbles. Your Member of Parliament.

And by Vincent too (for early on they had decided to keep in the family the quite generous annual grant of money that was available from the public funds to pay for an MP's secretarial and research needs). He became her trusty right-hand man, her amanuensis; also her fixer, political adviser, speechwriter, accountant. Together, in the constituency, they were a combination of GPs, parish priests, social workers, with a bit of something else, something rare and exciting.

Messengers from the outside world, from where the decisions were taken and the people who appeared on television every night and laid down the law spoke and dwelt. A breath of power in the air when Bubbles and Vincent came by. Power for good. After nine years, thousands of satisfied customers. They could hardly have done more.

And what good had it done *them*, Vincent thought, as he sat on the bed in his room, easing off his shoes. When the crunch came, when they needed every vote, where were those thousands? Some of them must have come out to scrawl their X's for Bubbles, but not enough. Not nearly enough. Ungrateful bastards. 2 a.m., 10 June 1983:

Anderson, T. (National Front) . . . 633
Bahadur, B.N. (Asian Workers Party) . . . 1,861
Johnson, R.J. (Labour) . . . 17,544
Leverton, C. Mrs (Conservative) . . . 1,729
McMorris, D. (Monster Raving Loony Party) . . . 247
Stabler, A. Mrs (SDP-Alliance) . . . 12,652

In the hall, Ron Johnson's lot had erupted in victory cheers, football chants, hoots of derision for the Stablers. Fights broke out in a couple of places. Their own people did not do well in them. The police had to clear a way through the taunting mob outside to get the Stablers to their car. A hate-filled bearded face appeared at Bubbles' window. It was Baz Jacobson, risen again from the murk and obscurity into which Bubbles' dominion in the constituency had briefly cast him. 'I hope you get cancer, you cunt,' he screamed.

And behold, after a dozen years, she had done just that.

Six

I

Whenever in those distant days I railed away against academic life and people, I meant always to make important exceptions. There are some men and women – I have known several – for whom scholarship and research are a constant, consuming joy. And however narrow and idiosyncratic their pursuits seem to me, I do always admire and envy this passion. Because he became involved in a curious fashion with the fates of both Goldy Stern and my brother Russell, I want to introduce at this point one of those fortunate people: I.E. Trasker, BA (Melbourne), Ph.D. (Cantab), author of numerous scholarly articles, and of one book, the monumental and definitive *Infrastructure of a Criminal Gang* (1976); much better known under the rather fanciful title of its popular edition: *The New Barabbas* (1978).

We – my wife Matty MacBride and I – first met Ivor Trasker in the mid-Sixties, about two months after we had moved to Cambridge, specifically when he stopped his car for us one Friday afternoon as we stood beside the A10, thumbs out, anxious as ever to escape from the windy city for a precious weekend in London. We discovered on our way down that he was working for the same advanced degree as myself, though in his case in sociology. Also, surprisingly, for we had not noticed him at any of the spartan and silent research students' dinners we'd attended, it turned out that he and I were attached to the same college. We became friends with Ivor on that journey down to London, and thereafter visited him quite frequently in Cambridge. Not entirely, I must admit, nor even especially for the simple pleasure of his company, but because, coming from his warm Australian homeland, he had taken the precaution to rent a flat with a central heating system efficient enough to defeat even the grotesquely cold Cambridge winters of that era. Many times when the weather got too much for us, when in fact my California-reared wife began to cry from the icy cold of our college flat, we crept over to Ivor's place. He was always there, usually studying when we arrived, but invariably welcoming. One of the few fond pictures from my personal scenes of married life is of the two of us at Ivor's glowing pad, each swathed in many thick sweaters and with our still-nerveless fingers wrapped tight around mugs of hot cocoa, listening dazedly while Ivor, in a short-sleeved shirt and light chinos, demonstrated with the aid of his wall map of Europe how there were no mountains, hardly even any hills, between the Russian Urals and English Cambridge, no natural barriers at all in fact to deflect and gentle the appalling Asiatic gales which, even as he spoke to us, were howling through the dark and shuttered streets outside.

I later learned that this 'nothing between here and the Urals' business was a standard piece of Cambridge folklore, brought out every winter to frighten new arrivals. But then it seemed only we three had spotted the phenomenon and grasped its import, and therefore Ivor's exposition had for us the force of revealed text. And how in those evenings we sat and drank our cocoa and smoked our dope and poured out our loathing of the frigid little city outside and its dreary people and draughty colleges and the whole benighted countryside beyond! At least my wife and I did; Ivor watched and listened and grinned at us and mostly held his peace.

Though one night he roused himself to give me the best piece of advice I heard in all my Cambridge experience. I'd been wittering on about whatever resentment was currently obsessing me – the idleness and superciliousness of my supervisor, perhaps, or the way they would turn you away from the university library if you'd forgotten to bring along your wretched little black scholar's gown. 'Oh for Christ's sake, Vince,' Ivor broke in at one point. 'What did you expect? You're nobody here, nor am I. We weren't even undergraduates here. We're on the lowest rung of all, and nobody gives a fuck about us. And what they especially don't give a fuck about is whether we give a fuck about them. *But* if you stick it out long enough, put up with all the nonsense, you'll come out with a degree that's money in the bank at any university anywhere in the world. It's your passport, man – what do you care about the bloody college grub? Jesus! Just stick it out.'

So I must have been going on about the lousy food the college served up at the formal dinners we were required to attend . . . Anyway there was enough good sense in this to keep me quiet for the rest of the evening. But it didn't stop Matty for a second – though to be fair she hadn't heard

Ivor's broadside in person, she'd been in the loo. In any case, by the next time we were round at his flat, I was back in harness, and sounding off same as always.

We two so hated Cambridge. I think it almost helped our marriage at the start, feeling this great shared passion. Though in the end, of course, it did a lot to destroy it, for Matty never forgave me for bringing her to the place. 'I was happy at Berkeley,' she used to wail to Ivor. And so she was, and so was I, and so why did we ever leave? There were no real professional or scholastic reasons for it. The standard of scholarship at Cambridge in my chosen field was high enough, but no better than at a dozen other places, at home or abroad. Snobbery was to blame in my decision, of course, and the chance to impress other people ever afterwards with the fact of having been – sort of – to Oxbridge.

But that was not the only, nor the main reason, I knew. Surely I had come here principally to please my parents. Always the beneficiary of the myth, I now at last started to become its victim. For my mother and father it was good when I became a London University undergraduate. It was very good. And then off to America: that impressed them a little too. But to see me at Cambridge! For they who had both left school at fourteen. For they who for all their lower middle-class English lives had been ruled, patronised, and lectured at by the ineffable, assertive products of Oxbridge. I think I never made them happier than when I wrote that I was going there.

Well, whatever joy my decision brought to my parents' house was not to be repeated when the time came and we moved into our college flat (up the Newmarket Road, hard by the gasworks). After a couple of weeks Matty had had enough. Our relationship, which had been born and flourished in the sunshine and against the background of San Francisco and the Golden Gate and the Pacific Ocean, started to wither and die under leaden skies, amidst the flat grey fields and icy blasts of East Anglia. (Although it's possible my memory exaggerates our malaise a little here. There must have been some contact still in those days, some loving moments together. I can't remember them now, but they must have happened, for practically on the last day of the academic year we discovered that she was pregnant.)

When Ivor Trasker and I left Cambridge – he with a much-admired Ph.D. thesis behind him, I with large promises to 'really get to grips with it over the summer' – we both got jobs at the same college of London University. I think he was a bit taken aback by our common achievement, for he had a pretty fair idea of just how hard I had worked on my dissertation (a drop in all the oceans compared to him). But in those brave days of university expansion, stranger appointments even than mine were being made, and whatever wry thoughts he may have had, he showed himself temperately but, I thought, genuinely pleased that our acquaintance was to continue.

Because our college was so big, because we were in different departments, because in any case Ivor was (and doubtless still is) a man dedicated to his work, with little time to spare for casual socialising, we did not often meet up in London. Sometimes though we ate lunch together, and it was on one of these occasions – about three years after our joint arrival in the capital, about twelve months after my wife's departure for her homeland in the company of our little daughter and a visiting linguistics professor from MIT (the latest in Matty MacBride's rather spectacular post-Cambridge series of affairs, intrigues, and one-night stands) – that over the corned beef and cress and sliced boiled beetroot in the faculty dining room, I happened to mention my acquaintance with Goldy Stern. Ivor, whose academic interests were focusing increasingly on the study of criminology, was immediately intrigued, and when, at his urging, I revealed how intimate was the line – running through my brother Russell – which connected me with the distinguished gangster and property developer, he could hardly contain his enthusiasm. At the end of the meal, he asked – actually he almost begged – for an introduction to Goldy. The hard pure light of scholarship was now burning in his usually mild and kindly eyes; and – because I had never really stopped admiring those who worshipped at the shrine, even though I could not be among them – I promised that I would try my best to arrange a meeting.

It proved not too difficult. Goldy, as I knew from his immediate and uncritical warmth towards me, was quite a snob in this area, and was only too happy to receive yet another bright young man from the university. I told him, nervously, that I thought Ivor might be wanting to meet him out of something more than mere curiosity; that he might even want to, well, study him. Goldy took the news complacently.

'We can deal with it, Vincent. We can listen to what he has to say. Can't we, honey?' And he awarded Val who sat beside him, her fabulous legs curled under her, one of his fondest squeezes.

So one evening I took Ivor down to Blackheath. The meeting had an awkward beginning when Johnny Blake, one of Goldy's young men, alertly knocked out of Ivor's hands the batch of 8×5 file cards which he had started to scribble on the moment he was over the threshold. But this little rumpus was soon forgotten. Goldy was at his most charming. His finest brandy was produced and it circulated a few times. Soon we were all smiling cheerfully at one another, good fellows all, scholars and gentlemen, the humour hardly wilting even when Ivor came to the point of the visit. His proposition was listened to carefully and, though some of Goldy's people were initially astonished that anyone could hope to make a living out of studying their activities, the gang on the whole was flattered by Ivor's request.

Goldy himself was clearly tempted. At one point he turned to me saying, 'It's all in the cause of scholarship, isn't it, Vincent?' I assured him that, as far as I was aware, it could not be anything else, and in that moment he seemed to make up his mind. He introduced again the name of his ex-statesman friend, our present university trustee. (I watched as Ivor, amazed, scribbled down the details of this connection.) 'If that busy man can find time for you chaps,' Goldy announced, 'I should damn well think I could do my bit.'

So it was arranged. Goldy and his men agreed to place themselves at Ivor's disposal for a three-month period. There would be a few simple questionnaires to fill out, but in the main it would only be a matter of the firm carrying on its usual activities, though now under the observation of a research team, headed of course by Ivor. In return, Ivor promised absolute anonymity and a half-dozen free copies of the resultant book. Some of the lads looked a bit glum at the scale of this reward; but Goldy was in such high spirits, so evidently pleased to be made a scholarly fuss of, that soon all doubts disappeared and they were ready to go along with whatever Ivor needed.

With the exception, I fear, of my brother Russell. Early on he had retired into the shadows and had watched the proceedings from then on with a look of tolerant contempt. As Goldy's brandy went round and the talk and laughter and boasts and promises mounted, it struck me powerfully once again what a difficult man my big brother was for anyone to use or patronise. Myself apart, of course.

II

Ivor moved competently about the business of setting up his project. His urgent entreaties conjured quite substantial sums out of our skinflint university's budget, and there were additional funds from the government's Social Research Council. And also, as I found out later, from a Sunday paper which contracted to buy up Ivor's findings from the study and turn them into exciting reading for their millions of readers. (They eventually appeared in three weekly parts under the overall title 'A City's Shame'.) Ivor was soon spending heftily, and his little office at the university became a sort of warehouse crammed full of items needed for the survey. This was still in the pre-personal computer age and the stuff he collected then would seem primitive now. There were the big cardboard boxes full of 8 × 5 cards of course, and smaller boxes of hard AB pencils, a dozen cassette tape-recorders, and several deep piles of questionnaires. In addition, Ivor had devoted quite a large slice of the budget to print up three thousand copies of a little four page brochure, describing the planned project, under the title *A Unique Survey*. The cover had a photo of himself in tweed sports jacket and corduroy trousers, smoking a briar pipe (though I must say I can't remember ever seeing him smoke anything in real life, except a joint once in a while back at Cambridge to keep Matty and me company). These booklets were destined for Ivor's academic colleagues, far and wide, known to him and unknown. He hired one of his research students at five bob an hour to address the envelopes, and for a couple of days the young scholar sat in Ivor's study, perched on a high stool, under a sign reading 'It Pays to Advertise' which Ivor had roguishly hung on his wall, directing the glossy brochures to sociology departments at universities the whole world over.

This young man – Alan Rice by name – and another called Jimmy Lewis formed the nucleus of Ivor's research effort. He described his technique to me – it may well have been a term common among social scientists in those Vietnam War days, presumably spreading from the discipline's heartland in American academe – as a 'creeping barrage'. For a couple of months Ivor, Alan and Jimmy worked by themselves in the libraries, concentrating on the job of getting the area of their future survey in focus. They studied South London geographically, demographically, politically, linguistically, medically. They looked, in the pages of books, journals, and government reports, at its schools, its churches, its parks, cinemas, public baths, bingo halls, prisons, cemeteries. They had a great map of the area on the wall which they all laboured to commit to memory. It was like a gathering of prospective taxi drivers on 'the Knowledge' in Ivor's study sometimes.

'Commercial Way, Peckham to Nunhead railway station?'

'Right on Peckham Hill Street, left on the High Street, into Queen's Road, right on Lugard Road, into Holydale, all the way down, and bob's your uncle.'

Ivor used a part of his grant to purchase a chic-looking, Italian-made slide projector and borrowed a wide white screen from the Art History people downstairs. The three social scientists spent much time in the darkened study staring at the images of South London scenes and people thrown up on the screen. I watched with them a couple of times, but there was something about Ivor's treatment of his subject matter on these occasions which drove me away. South-of-the-river then was still largely undiscovered territory for the middle classes of the capital. Certainly, for me, Ivor's approach to the population of one half of the city had something of the unconsciously patronising enthusiasm of an early anthropologist set down among a Stone Age tribe in Amazonia. And after all, as I could not help reminding myself while I watched the people on the screen, I sprang from this tribe myself. As did my parents, and my brother too.

I was present though on one occasion when Ivor was putting up some photos he'd specially taken of Goldy and the rest of the firm. He ran fairly quickly through the various younger gangsters, most of whom had assumed would-be humorous poses for Ivor's camera (Mikey Fanshaw, like an idiot, pointing a toy revolver at his head). Ivor delivered his brief comments on each of the firm as their pictures came up and I could hear his research team (by now grown to a dozen young men and women) scratching away in their notebooks by the light of tiny reading lamps. Then the projector clicked and a picture of my Russell (taken without his knowledge?) appeared. Ivor's voice became animated at this point:

'I really want you to watch out for this one. This bloke Russell is the one potentially volatile element in our community, the only one capable, I believe, of dividing group loyalties. Now at the moment he appears to accept his subordinate role and uses his strengths to reinforce the authority of the leader. He may well not stay in this mode. He may want to set up on his own, or he may even want to take over. Then again he could just stay as he is. It'll be interesting in the course of this study to see which way this one breaks.' Ivor paused to allow the scribbling pens to catch up with him. Then continued: 'In any case, we should watch him carefully if only for the sake of our follow-up study. He's clearly a man with a considerable future. In or out of this mob.'

In the dark, I gazed fearfully up at the larger-than-life replica of my brother's calm ironic features. A considerable future. Was it really so?

Seven

I

When the phone rang, Vincent, dozing, had been inter-mittently aware that his mind, in its semi-detached state, was going down a list of all the women he had ever made love to. Considering the free-and-easy times he had lived in and the promiscuous generation he belonged to, it was not a long list. Including wives, the number could exactly be counted on the fingers and thumb of one hand. So far he had got through Margot from Inverness, who he'd met on a hitchhiking trip to France when he was eighteen, and Sarah Aitchison, first year at college, who had unluckily broken her ankle on the way downstairs from his room after an afternoon in bed. The date ended up in the UC Hospital casualty; it turned out to be their last, at her request. Not that she blamed him exactly, but . . .

He groped his way across the counterpane to the bedside table. Scrabbled to find his reading glasses and put them on before he picked up the telephone. It was an old habit, Bubbles had always found it funny. It came out of their time in active politics together. A phone call for him almost always meant business then, which meant having to write something down. Hence the glasses. Since their ejection from the political life, he had managed to break himself of the searching-for-a-biro side of the equation.

'It's Jack,' said the voice at the other end of the line. 'Jack Rolls.'

'Jack. Good Lord!' Vincent breathed. 'I – I hardly—'

Expected to hear from you. Not just right now, at any time in the whole future of the world. But really, as he controlled the agitation that hearing from Jack Rolls – Jack Rolls! – would naturally create in him, Vincent marvelled at the fact that he should happen to hear from his one-time friend and ally at just such a time. When he happened to be touring his modest harem of past wives and girlfriends. It was quite extraordinary. And funny. Though he couldn't expect Jack to appreciate the joke.

'How are you, Jack?' Vincent said, trying to keep his tone light and neutral.

Before its virtual takeover by the Left, Jack and Audrey Rolls had been leading Labour Party lights in the constituency Bubbles represented. In fact their influence considerably pre-dated her arrival. At least Jack's did. As an idealistic young GP he had deliberately chosen after qualifying to join a practice in one of the most deprived areas of London. This would have been in around '53, '54 – about the time Goldy Stern was laying the foundations of the first of his major tower blocks, which was erected in fact only a few streets away from where Jack was now working. How exactly the two had become acquainted Vincent wasn't sure. Not on a directly professional basis, he was pretty certain. Like many ambitious South Londoners, however patriotic, Goldy preferred to select his professional advisers from north-of-the-river. His lawyers were up there, likewise his architect, interior decorator, chiropractor and accountant. And Vincent had certainly heard him more than once mention proudly that he was going to have to go up to Harley Street to have some minor ailment seen to (they were always minor: apart from a chronic lower-back pain, Goldy enjoyed excellent health until his sudden death from heart failure, at home in Blackheath in 1981).

Yet it was probably through Jack's work that they had met all the same. A lot of the men that came down – from Ireland, the north of England, Scotland – to work on Goldy's project would have found their way to Jack's nearby practice. Vincent had heard from someone – he wasn't sure who, perhaps it was Russell – that safety conditions on Goldy's early sites had not been all that good. 'Rough and ready' was the phrase he remembered. There had been some bother about it among what were termed the 'malcontents' on the labour force. Some of the doctors who'd had to deal with the results of on-site accidents began to speak out. Complaints reached the ears of the authorities. The health and safety inspectors became involved. There was talk of shutting down the whole project. It would have bankrupted Goldy almost before he'd got started.

Vincent was unsure exactly how the matter had been resolved. Except that one day the inspectors had been withdrawn, and in their place a working party had been established with the remit to look into safety standards in the construction industry throughout the borough. Represented on this committee: management, unions, borough council-lors, local clergy and GPs (one of the latter almost certainly Jack Rolls, though Vincent had never thought to establish the fact). Its report was long delayed; in fact the block was completed and Goldy's operations had moved to another borough entirely by the time it came out, and so he could not be damaged materially by its rather damning conclusions. Another development of the time was that the lease of the little two-storey building on the High Street which the local Labour Party inhabited was bought and presented to the members collectively by a benefactor who wished to remain anonymous.

'It was me,' Goldy had confided to Vincent during one of their late-night talkfests in Fulham. 'And that was just the start of it. You wouldn't believe what I had to shell out to that bunch: office equipment, election expenses, cases of champers for the Christmas raffle, fact-finding missions to the South of France . . . Oh, they lived high off the hog with me, I can tell you. I was glad to get out of that borough. Anybody want an interest-free loan, muggins was right there. In fact, I was lucky if it got called a loan. Either way it was the same, I hardly ever saw the dosh again.'

'Seriously?'

'Absolutely. The bloody agent, feller called Stevens – he had his hand so deep in my pocket it was indecent. And even worse than him was this bloke Jack Rolls, a doctor would you believe? But I had to pay up. Hush money, you might say. Those bloody micks were always falling off the scaffolding.'

At the time the name of Jack Rolls meant nothing to Vincent; but a year or so later, after he had met the Rollses, and had heard Jack's account of his personal political development, he had been keen to challenge Goldy's version of events.

'Jack only lost his socialist idealism in the late Sixties. It was Harold Wilson that did it. But before that – I can't believe he would be so cynical as to—'

'I know what I know,' Goldy had insisted. 'And I'm not talking about the Sixties. I'm talking about 1954 . . . Jack Rolls. Biggest crook in the manor. You be careful around him.'

'Fancy hearing from you, Jack,' Vincent said now.

'It seemed appropriate,' Jack grated out in the gravelly tones that years of dedicated cigar smoking and whisky drinking had bestowed upon the rather light and melodious voice that Vincent remembered from their first acquaintance.

'How do you mean?'

'Wake up, man,' the other barked. 'What do you think I mean? It's appropriate because the Great She-Elephant has at last reached the sacred graveyard.'

'Actually it's not till tomorrow. And she's being cremated. And I must say, Jack, that I find that a rather unattractive way of describing my wife. The extra weight was only really a factor in her last years, you know; and it had all pretty much faded away by the time she—'

'I was talking metaphorically, you idiot. Have you lost what few brains you ever possessed?'

'You're definitely being offensive now, Jack. And at such a time. Are you drunk?'

'That's good. That makes me laugh. *I'm* being offensive? You adulterous bastard, Stabler.'

Audrey Rolls had been no spring chicken when Vincent and Bubbles had first met her, a few weeks prior to the adoption meeting in 1974. At thirty-one, she was nineteen years younger than her husband; yet she carried this hardly unprecedented age-gap as if it was a unique burden, bravely borne in the face of stern, unrelenting fate. She was always having to hurry home to see that Jack was all right: 'he can't be left by himself for ten minutes at a time'. She was always stopping him doing things, picking things up for him, interrupting him when he was in the full flow of discourse to ask if he was tired, if he needed a rest, a warm drink, a cushion, his medicine. When he was allowed to speak at any length, Audrey would listen with exaggerated attention, breaking in occasionally to explain some particular turn of phrase – 'that's Jack's generation's way of putting it; what *we* would say is . . .' and so on – as if her husband had just stepped off the plane from New Guinea with only a few sentences of pidgin English with which to make his way in the modern world.

Bubbles and Vincent found her completely dreadful in the first weeks of their acquaintance. They used to escape from an evening with the Rollses – there were several, Jack and Audrey being so powerful within the Party then and their support, pre- the adoption meeting, worth cultivating – exclaiming once alone at her awfulness and her poor husband's dire fate in being tethered to her. It took some time to notice that Jack quite enjoyed Audrey's attentions, and was inclined to become testy if they were withdrawn to any degree. Even though it was plain that he actually needed none of them; that, for instance, so far from being unable to spend ten minutes alone, what he loved above all, as he confided to Vincent once in the pub after a branch meeting, was to spend an evening in an armchair with a glass of Scotch, a cigar, and a paperback novel, preferably of the post-war, far-flung, masculine type: John Masters, Nicholas Montserrat, Nevil Shute, Alistair MacLean. It was an early bond between Jack and Vincent when they discovered that they shared a regard (somewhat covert in Vincent's case) for the Hornblower saga.

In time the Stablers concluded that Jack's need for all this pampering was the result of a seriously disappointed ego. Life had not worked out for him at all; his star had dimmed to the merest pinprick of light in the dark, there being a ton of difference between a brilliant young doctor flamboyantly denying himself worldly success in order to serve the humblest of London's poor and an ageing and unnoticed general practitioner stuck in the same practice he had started out with, while his nimbler contemporaries at medical school were all rising to the heights of the profession. Nobody was interested now in Jack Rolls' great humanitarian sacrifice; nobody really was even aware of it any more, and so the only reward he would ever know was the joy of having done good to his fellow man, which by the time the Stablers met him was of no interest to him at all.

'I could have been the Queen's Gynaecologist,' he had mourned one night to Vincent during a particularly boozy session at 'Blushes', a wine bar, the first attempt to establish such a concern in Bubbles' constituency (it did not last). 'I could have had a knighthood.'

'But you're not a gynaecologist, Jack,' Vincent had explained patiently. 'You're a GP.'

'Never mind that. I knew the fellow who *is* the Queen's Gynaecologist when we were medical students, and he was a complete fucking dolt; used to crib from me all the time.'

But 'Sir' Jack Rolls was clearly out of the question by now. No schools of medicine or clinics or foundations would ever be named after him, not even a ward, not even at the local hospital (doomed to close in any case in one of the cuts of 1983), where he was known generally as 'Old Fingers' because of a certain tactile appreciation he had liked to demonstrate towards the younger female nurses, until a senior registrar had called him into his office and informed him that times had changed and his habits had better do the same, otherwise he would not be welcome on the premises.

From the Queen's Gynaecologist to Old Fingers; such a comedown, such ingratitude. Only Audrey, in Jack's eyes, gave him the consideration and appreciation that he felt the whole world owed him.

Looking back long afterwards it seemed to the Stablers that it was probably only at the time they first met him that Jack had begun to understand how deep was the hole that he had dug for himself. That what he was now he would always be. That there would be no eleventh-hour rescues, and he was not, after all, a hero of his time. For a couple more years there were no great changes, but after that his deterioration was marked. The drinking, solitary and con-vivial, became unbridled. Then it was that his voice took on its later gravelly rasp. His appearance changed too. Still in his fifties he seemed almost like an old man suddenly. He moved about slowly and effortfully. His hair thinned drastically, his eyes became veiny and perplexed. Now it was that he might have had real need for a bit of care and cheering up from a devoted partner. At which point Audrey Rolls, rather late in the day, discovered her feminist needs and responsibilities and declined to spend any more time on the care and protection of her husband.

'I have given years of my life to running after that old fool,' she told the Stablers one night when they were driving her home from the hospital (Jack had gashed his arm rather badly in a tipsy midnight attempt to put up some shelves in his study; he was being kept on the casualty ward overnight for observation; the Rolls's car was out of commission because Jack had earlier bashed a front wheel out of alignment getting the vehicle out of the garage). 'I have played the dutiful daughter with him; so dutiful that I even slept with him. I have allowed myself to be sucked entirely into his patriarchal empire. Enough. Enough!'

It was very dramatic. Vincent's contention was that the violence of Audrey's new opinions was exactly a result of her previous docility and self-denial. He was on slightly dangerous ground here for it could be argued that Bubbles had shown much the same qualities in a former period of her life. She too had been a self-effacing, self-sacrificing wife once, though not with Vincent of course. But it seemed to him that Bubbles, when her time came, was able to shed her former self quite quietly and without fuss, like the butterfly from the chrysalis, as if the strong and unafraid person she became had always existed within, only requiring circumstances to bring her forth.

Audrey, however, shot out of her former disguise in all directions, like puffed wheat. Actually, in those noisy, histrionic months when she was discovering the woman within the wimp, the Stablers had finally concluded that the Audrey–Jack combination, that she was now so bitterly repudiating, had been very much a *folie-à-deux*, that she as much as he had been playing roles in the same daft scenario, in her case to be the muse and inspiration of the brilliant doctor who sacrifices everything, etcetera, etcetera. The revelation, too long delayed, of the fatuousness of this dream affected her as much as him. The sleepers awake and turn nasty. A few years of intensive counselling were probably the best bet for both of them. Or failing that, just a few years might do it – the simple passage of time might bring if not solutions, at least weariness and apathy to the tortured couple. Always supposing they did not break up in the meantime. Which of course is what eventually happened.

But after all none of this explained why, after several years of problematic, sometimes intimate, but always chaste friendship, a certain autumn afternoon in the early Eighties should have found Audrey Rolls and Vincent Stabler sharing a bed in a small seaside hotel, located on a backstreet some way from the front, in order, as Jack subsequently put it, to 'screw your disgusting brains out'. Coincidentally their respective spouses were also at about that time to be found together in another hotel bedroom in the same town, though in their case – as Jack also liked often to point out – not for any purposes that happened to be lewd, treacherous, or degrading.

II

'What the hell could she have seen in you?' Jack Rolls rasped down the phone. 'I never could understand it.'

'Jack, it's just not worth raking over all those old—'

'I mean it was obvious the silly bitch was planning to screw *somebody*. Mainly to make me miserable if she could. But why *you*? Unemployed loafer from Penge, Cambridge-reject – and those dons knew what they were doing, by the way – plain as a pikestaff to boot—'

There were so many misstatements of fact in this tirade that it was hard to know where to begin correcting them. Vincent closed his eyes, gripped the instrument in his hand more tightly.

'Jack, it's so pointless going on like this. What more can we say? I've apologised so many times. To you. To Bubbles. What happened at that hotel should never have happened. And given that it did, it should never have been revealed to you two. I still can't understand Audrey's motive. You – I can see she'd have wanted to hurt you. But I always thought she liked Bubbles, I do think she liked her . . .' Vincent drew a deep breath. 'Also, Jack, on another of your points: I'd like to point out that this all happened over sixteen years ago.'

'So what?'

'Well, for one thing: whatever my appearance is now, I think you'll admit that so far from being "plain as a pikestaff", I was not actually so bad to look at in those days. I had all my hair, my teeth; and I had a spring in my step then, a ready smile, an air of *joie de vivre* in fact. Audrey used to remark on it. She found it most attractive. I was busy, happy, *engaged* in those days. Women flocked to me.'

'You pathetic ass, Stabler.'

At this point, to Vincent's relief, for he was finding the

conversation increasingly tedious and futile, the phone rang to interrupt it. He groped his way across the counterpane to the bedside table. Found his glasses and put them on and picked up the receiver. It was Rob at the other end. Vincent's heart glowed. To hear his son's voice again after a long silence. It was natural. Then he remembered that it hadn't been so long; he had spoken to Rob only yesterday. He shook his head to clear away the remnants of sleep.

'Rob. What's happening?'

'Dad, I was just saying, I'm still at Heathrow. We got in an hour late. In case you were worrying.'

Vincent turned the digital clock towards him. It showed 7:10 p.m.

'No, it's OK. I was sleeping.'

He would have said more then but he remembered suddenly the import of their last conversation and, for the moment, the memory silenced him. Vincent had had to confess yesterday to having taken a somewhat rash decision. And taken it many times. For he had found himself so infuriated by the meagre public notice Bubbles' passing had caused that he had resolved on the spot to make tomorrow's funeral service completely private. Thereafter whenever people rang to ask him when and where it was taking place, he had told them no service, and whatever minimal formalities would have to be got through in the way of disposing of Bubbles' remains would be private, family only. Flowers by request to the local hospice which had been involved in her case in the last few months. He would be so grateful, Vincent had added, if these wishes could be passed on to anyone else the caller thought might be planning to attend.

'I just didn't want them there,' he had told Rob yesterday. 'Looking at their watches, mouthing all that sympathy crap. None of them bothered with her when she was alive. Not much anyway. Not for the last year or two. But do you mind? Do you think Bubbles would have minded? I can phone them back.'

He had felt, even as he was speaking, how Rob was pulling away from him. Fending him off. Never forgiving him. And yet nothing personal exactly. He'd always thought Rob might even like him quite a bit. It was all – what had happened long ago – just unforgivable.

He'd heard Rob sigh. 'I'm sure Mum wouldn't mind. And I certainly don't.'

'It'll be fine with just us two, won't it?'

'Sure it will, Dad.'

(Could have been three. Ought to be three. He had resisted an impulse to ask if Tim had any plans to show up. Pointless. Completely. Tim hadn't been near his mother for nearly thirteen years. Even her death was not going to change that.)

'We few, we happy few?'

'Right,' said Rob, and had rung off soon after.

'Did I wake you, Dad?' he said now. 'I'm sorry.'

'No, it's all right. I'm glad you did. I was having a stupid conversation with old Jack Rolls. Remember him?'

There was silence from the other end.

'Surely you do. Him and Audrey were always over at the house when you and Tim were kids. Remember? They separated when you were about – oh, well, eighteen. You would have moved out by then. Though Tim was still around, I guess. Anyway Audrey went off to South Africa in the end. Last we heard she had re-married and was working as a reflexologist in Capetown.'

'Dad, you were having a conversation with Jack Rolls?'

'Well, more like he was shouting abuse and I was having to listen to it.'

Another silence, and then: 'I'll be with you soon as I can, Dad. You just sit down, make yourself a cup of tea.'

'Righty-ho,' said Vincent and hung up. He went straight down to the kitchen. He had picked up some smoked salmon and brown bread on his visit to Safeway yesterday. Rob's favourite snack. Add some sliced cucumber, water-cress, put it between some slices of brown bread, perfect. And bound to be needed. The crap the airlines served was neither tasty nor filling. Unless it had improved in the three years since Vincent had last taken to the skies – accompanying Bubbles to a conference held at Marburg University in Germany on boosting the representation of women in European legislative bodies. It turned out that the organisers, who had paid for air fares and hotel accommodation for both Stablers, were under the impression that she was still a member of the British parliament and were extremely fed up to discover they had fallen short in their calculations by more than a dozen years. But Bubbles didn't let this bother her. She spoke out forcefully and often on the subjects under debate. She was equally energetic and successful at socialising among her fellow delegates in the college bars and cafés after each day's work was done. On the last night, almost the whole conference had gone to celebrate in a vast 'contemporary' beer-hall in the old town.

When the karaoke sound system broke down, Bubbles had led the throng – Germans and French and Dutch and Croats, and practically every other nationality under the European sun – in belting out a medley of Seekers' hits. 'Morningtown Ride'. 'A World of Our Own'. 'I Know I'll Never Find Another You'. Her swollen body had teetered on the edge of the bench she stood on, her eyes were closed, her massive arms upraised; she had swayed in time with the singing:

> High above the dawn is waiting,
> And my tears are falling rain,
> For the carnival is over,
> We may never meet again.

Vincent had been so proud of her.

Eight

I

At last Ivor Trasker's 'creeping barrage' crept up to a crescendo, and the troops went in. Every morning the students quit their squalid, multi-occupant lairs in Ladbroke Grove, Camden Town, or Hackney (and Ivor left his pleasant, three-bedroom apartment in Canonbury) to make their way into the wilderness beyond the river. Loaded down with their clipboards, file cards, and recording machines, each attached himself to one of Goldy's people (Ivor himself took on the near-inseparable trio of Goldy, Val, and Russell), and trailed their subjects throughout the day and usually far into the night.

Ivor required his assistants to enter each day's activities in minute detail on their observation sheets. A few hours' entries on one of these sheets might run: '10.06–11.15: in Rube's Café, Malham Road, Forest Hill. Subject had two teas, one Penguin biscuit. Read *Mirror*, *Sun*. Refused offer of my *Black Dwarf*. 11.48–12.16: Entrance to Catford Bridge Station. Subject explained that girlfriend might be turning up there around noon. She didn't. 12.40–1.02: Balham Hill. Subject collected a TV set and three Kenwood mixers from the back door of Wilton's Electrical and Hardware. 1.25–2.04: William Hill betting shop, Balham High Road. Subject put two pounds on Stray No More (two-thirty at Lincoln) and another three on Bonnie's Girl (three o'clock at Doncaster), and ten shillings on Student Prince in the same race for me. None of them paid off.'

Each assistant's assignment was permanent for the duration of the study; he remained with the same firm member all the time. In consequence, several quite close friendships sprung up among these observer–subject, student–gangster combinations. At first Goldy's people looked on Ivor's with wary eyes indeed. Neville 'Sniffer' Clark complained that his shadow did nothing but hang about, smiling vaguely, and sighing 'What a trip!' to all of his (Sniffer's) attempts to be friendly. 'Black Nick' Gobelins twice had to thump his researcher for thrusting International Socialist literature on several of his (Nick's) friends, family, and customers, and addressing them as 'Comrades'. From both sides (though rather timidly from Ivor's people) there were the obvious digs about clothing and hairstyles. But once these early barriers had been negotiated, the all day, every day nature of the relationship began to have its effect. The researcher became a familiar part of the scenery. He was someone who shared intimately in the vast boredoms and petty interests of the gangster's day. It came so that if a researcher was off sick, very often his subject would be clearly restless and distracted all through that day, not to be settled in himself again until the college-boy had returned and the twosome re-established. (By the way, it was always college-*boy*; to a man the gangsters flatly refused to be followed around all day by a girl-student – 'some fucking tart'. They felt – and were convincing in conveying their fears – that they would lose serious face in the community if they let that happen. In those still politically incorrect days there was little attempt by the project leader to combat this sexism. The young women initially recruited for Ivor's team were mostly replaced by young men; one or two were allowed to remain back at base, collating the data as it flowed in from the field, and typing up the audio interviews.)

In all these relationships it was a case of Goldy's people taking Ivor's under their wings, an elder/younger brother thing. It could hardly be otherwise. Early on, the members of the firm had been outraged to discover that most of these young scholars, even those with teaching responsibilities, even those with children, were trying to support life on an income that averaged around £700 a year. The pallor and slovenliness of their shadows' appearances, the frequency with which they took sick-days, and the ease with which even the undemanding nature of a gangster's schedule seemed to tire them – all of which Goldy's people had first put down to a kind of class-based congenital deficiency – were now explained. Generously, Goldy's men set themselves to feeding up their researchers, anxiously watching as the college-boys spooned down enormous meaty and suety meals at their expense each day. Like prostitutes taking pride in the pimp's clothes and jewels, they vied with each other as to who could display the liveliest, plumpest, best turned-out researcher. Goldy's men bought their observers gifts too: a silk tie, a cigarette lighter, cuff-links (and then, necessarily, a shirt with the sleeves designed to take them). Researchers with young families would often make their journeys home across the river laden with boxes of sweets for the kids, and toys and comics, and something special for the wife or girlfriend too. And their patrons went even further than that. An angry deputation appealed to Goldy about the wretched pay of their observers. They threatened non-cooperation with the survey unless it was immediately adjusted upwards. Goldy, himself genuinely appalled when he learned of the current scale of payment, hurried to consult with Ivor. He returned shaking his head.

'It's all fair and above board,' he told the deputation. 'Ivor tells me it's all he's got in the kitty. Education's being starved of funds. That's why he can't pay his people properly. Blame the Heath government, lads; Ivor's doing what he can.'

Nevertheless, the deputation persisted and in the end, after much pressure, which included, I believe, several hardly-concealed threats to his own health and safety, Ivor came up with a final offer of an extra 13p an hour per researcher. To do this he would have to cancel plans to produce and distribute another publicity brochure – called 'Half-Way There', cover showing Ivor on top of the Post Office Tower looking down towards the distant brown smear on the skyline that represented South London. Rather against the advice of their militant champions, the researchers accepted the deal.

In return for these many kind services, the researchers found, to their sorrow, that there was nothing really of any value they had to offer – except their company. And, involuntarily, their women. One or two of Goldy's people, who had made special chums of their observers, penetrated early on into the squatting and bedsitter territories north of the river. Soon channels of communication were opened up with a number of university colleges and parties and brunches at Goldy's Blackheath castle (not at all to the pleasure of Val and other native female veterans) were overrun with girl students, excitedly fishing in the strange, gangland waters. Goldy's young men entirely approved of the incursion, though sometimes they were made a bit nervous by the new breed's uninhibited (post-Pill, pre-Aids, and just about pre-feminist) approach. Indeed it was a strange sight to see one of these large, brilliant girls, fresh down from Yorkshire or Humberside, with her four good passes at A-level, her tits free and easy under her T-shirt, and her labial divide tightly defined by her Levi's, backing little Sniffer Clark or Johnny Blake against a wall, hissing into a twitching ear 'You're so fooking fabulous – ah want to fook you senseless, me!'

This sort of thing did cause distinct though temporary rifts in the observer–subject partnerships though. At these parties, throughout all this gamy foreplay, the little knot of college-boys would herd defensively over by the bar, sipping beer and smoking dope, self-consciously ignoring the antics of their wives and girlfriends as each scented out, hunted down, and finally made off with the gangster of her choice. But by the following Monday invariably the difficulty appeared to be forgotten. The matched pairs set off again on their rounds with just as much cordiality as they had finished up the previous Friday. Indeed, I think there was a certain amount of vicarious pride taken by the students in their women's conquests.

'Debbie's had Nick Gobelins *and* Stewie Dunn *and* Johnny Blake,' I overheard one Ph.D. student boasting about his wife. 'Not bad, eh?' he'd added with wistful pride.

II

The hard truth was that the usual daily round of one of Goldy's young men, though not tiring, was quite exceptionally dull. His primary duty was to be available. And since Goldy, under pressure from my brother, was increasingly putting his main effort into his more legitimate businesses, the services of his young men were that much less in demand. Indeed, they were becoming almost purely formal and ceremonial. Goldy liked to be surrounded by some muscle when he went out clubbing. Or attended boxing 'promotions' up north (Hackney, Finsbury Park, Highbury). But apart from this, his boys had few regular duties. They spent their days wandering around South London on foot or in their cars – to a man, they despised public transport – dropping off at regular intervals at the same old familiar caffs, pubs, amusement arcades and betting shops. Once in a while, they'd phone in to Goldy's castle to be told, usually by Russell, that there was nothing on, not to worry, they weren't needed. Once a week, at Goldy's regular Sunday brunch, they'd turn up to collect their week's pay: about forty quid on average, tax-free of course. Only rarely can they have felt they had earned it. For only rarely now did the call ever come to them, late at night or early in the morning, to get in their motors and roar out to some club across the river or mansion in North Kent or council flat in Southwark to settle the hash of whoever had been so foolish as to arouse Goldy's wrath. This was what they had all joined the organisation to do; yet by now such episodes constituted merely a brief, very occasional relief in an otherwise tame and monotonous existence.

Naturally this lack of excitement became even more irksome in the presence of the academic researchers. It was clear from the timid deference and tense excitement they showed initially around the gangsters that Ivor's young helpers had great hopes for this study, that – much like me whenever I entertained Goldy in my flat – they expected heaped helpings of burglary, extortion, beatings and murder. When in fact the reality of a gangster's life revealed itself to be a rather tedious wandering around the backstreets of South London their disappointment was keen and was quickly sensed – and resented – by their subjects. It was taxing enough for hard men like Black Nick Gobelins or Johnny Blake to have to endure their daily rounds, much worse to see them written down – '10.58–11.07: Dropped into Woolworths, Peckham High Street; purchase 40 Benson & Hedges, and two 60-watt light bulbs. 11.08–11.45: Peckham High Street; standing around' – on his observer's cards. And it seems to have often happened that a gang member, seeing his life set out in such prosaic terms would become restless, and might well ultimately seek to spice up his personal 8 × 5 cards a bit. A new swagger would show in his deportment, a new roughness in his voice. Soon quite conventional errands would become invested with an air of violence and danger, and bookies and pub-owners who, for old times'-sake mostly, had been paying thirty bob a fortnight protection money to Goldy for years, would find themselves being visited on collection day by a young man transformed from his usual polite and deferential self into a hulking tough, snarling menaces over the counter out of the corner of his mouth, and accompanied mysteriously by another, hairier young man, who throughout the visit scribbled busily upon a clipboard.

Or again, it rather often happened that a subject, confronted with some such item on a questionnaire as: 'Do you carry a gun regularly in your work?' would not only, out of a desire to impress his observer, answer the question falsely in the affirmative, but would also begin to agitate with Goldy for the right to carry a firearm. Only too often the request was apparently granted and a few days afterwards the researcher's eyes would be gratified by a sight of the bulge of a pistol worn on their subject's hip, or in a homemade shoulder holster.

(Though I spoke to Russell about this once, for it seemed a wholly novel and undesirable development in the way Goldy operated, and he swore to me that only one of these recent requests to be allowed to tool-up had ever been granted, and that on a temporary basis only and because the man in question lived on an estate where a West Indian gang was currently entrenching themselves and he needed something to impress them with. In other words, Russell said, the guns that were brought out to thrill Ivor's researchers were always the same gun, passed along from gangster to gangster.)

Nevertheless, the number of violent incidents involving gang members rose notably in the first weeks of the survey. There was a stabbing in a club in Streatham. A man was beaten badly and pushed out of a moving car in Cutt Street near the river. Guns (in the plural, I never checked with Russell about this incident) were waved around by Goldy's men in an argument in a Lambeth pub. And when these happenings were reported back to Blackheath, they seemed almost always to have a completely trivial cause which bore no relation to the level of violence employed.

I don't know how much Goldy worried about this development. In many ways I think he liked it. He had not been, I guessed, entirely easy with the increasing respectability and placidity of his life; part of him seemed to hanker after the rough old days and the brutal methods with which he had started to build his fortune. He liked very much I know to sit around yarning with his boys, encouraging them to share their murky little adventures blow by blow, and investing them with much more glamour than they were worth. I think this made him feel better, stronger, still virile. He liked to feel he had control of such tough young men.

Russell, I knew, felt very differently. He had not been happy with Ivor and his survey from the start. And, he revealed to me one day, he was truly concerned with the survey's day-to-day effects on the gang, the B-movie fantasies that it bred in them. He feared there was a reckoning in store unless things improved. And he blamed Goldy for allowing it all to happen in the first place.

'I can't help feeling sometimes,' my brother told me once, 'that the guvnor's gone soft in the head.' At the time we were in the Jaguar sports model that he'd just bought, at a very reasonable price, from a showroom off the Wandsworth Road in which Goldy had an interest. We were *en route* from Blackheath to my place, and he was negotiating the big roundabout at the Elephant & Castle. Other cars fell away from us as if bowing us through. Secretly I was trying to see their drivers' expressions, hoping to catch them paying homage to my brother's lordly progress.

Of course I liked the idea that I might be included in their regard. A splash of reflected glory. It would have been, I remember thinking, a fine thing if we had been captured at that moment on a bit of film, or better a photograph. What would you have called such a picture? *The Stabler Brothers – Going Places?* We could have sent it to our parents (still both alive at this date, though our father had just had his first stroke). They would have put it on the mantelpiece, next to our baby pictures, and Russell's wedding day, and his sons' baby pictures, and me setting off for my first term at Cambridge.

Nine

I

He was standing on the threshold, smiling the neutral sort of smile that seemed to have been his trademark ever since the first time he had come home on leave from the Army. Neutral, easygoing, detached. Up to that point it had been all struggle with Rob. Inside school he fought his teachers, in the playground and streets he fought the other children. At home he terrorised his younger brother. Around his mother he was noisy, angry, disobedient. Towards Vincent he maintained a correct but watchful posture. When he spoke to his new father, which was only when he had to, he was polite, distant. Vincent though was sure he could detect always a trailing note of irony and even menace in the boy's careful speech.

'I'm afraid I'm going to wake up one morning and find he's beaten me to death with a hammer,' he complained to Bubbles, just before their marriage, as they lay in bed in her house.

'He's just a little boy,' she scoffed. 'He's only eleven.'

'He's growing all the time,' Vincent worried into the pillow.

(Ironically, considering later events, it was only Rob's reaction to the situation that had concerned them at first. Tim, by contrast, seemed to be very calm and accepting of it.

Though there were doubts for a time whether he completely understood it, for he would quite frequently ask his mother when Vincent would be going back to his own home.)

'Gosh, you're looking fine, Rob,' Vincent glowed now when he'd led his son into the sitting-room. 'Fit and tanned . . . You're looking so well!'

'Why shouldn't I be?'

'Well, you know—' Vincent put on an exaggeratedly fearful tone to disguise the real fear he always felt whenever he contemplated Rob's vocation. 'Coming from a war-zone.'

'But that's all over, Dad. Pretty much. For the time being. Didn't you hear? Both sides have declared peace. Kiss and make up. Happened last year?'

Vincent felt a momentary stir of panic – he had not the least idea what his son was talking about . . . Then he relaxed.

'Of course we heard. Your mother was so relieved. Nobody would be taking potshots at her boy any more.'

'Oh, it was always pretty safe where I was. I used to tell her that.'

'The Army takes special care of its PE Instructors, eh?'

'That's it.'

'Government-issue trainers with homing devices in the soles and explosive laces?'

'No comment.'

There was a note of easy banter between them. It had not always been so when they talked of what Vincent had learned to think of as Rob's 'cover'. (Bubbles claimed never to have believed in it from the first, though Vincent had his doubts about that.) For two years Rob had been based out in

Germany performing normal duties with his infantry regiment, as far as they knew. Bubbles had learned to get over her initial disappointment that he had gone into the Army.

'He could have gone to university,' she told her husband. 'He could have gone to Cambridge. You could have got him in.'

'Not sure about that.'

But she was so pleased by the transformation the Army had wrought in her oldest boy – the surly, slovenly, uncooperative teenager turned into a polite, accommodating, neatly turned-out young man – that she learned to stifle her objections. She was delighted when he told them he had received his first promotion, then his next. He was clearly doing well, and looked so well on it, how could she criticise the choice he had made? Vincent, after his initial relief at the metamorphosis, found himself at times detecting something a bit odd and unreal about Rob's new manner. Sometimes he wondered indeed if it was all an act. But he could see no purpose to the performance, if it was one. Certainly it was always consistent, never wavered. His suspicions died away, remained only as a trace at the very back of his mind. And if they came suddenly to the fore, late at night, early in the morning, when he lay wakeful beside Bubbles, he was able to shrug them aside. Better this version of Rob, than the other. Much better. And if there was an element of pretence – why? why? was he laughing at them? – it was best to ignore it. Make no challenges. They had to accept it, whatever he chose to offer them. Now they had lost the other child – other *children*, he remembered, acknowledging always a second or two late the little girl who had been taken away from him – Rob was all the family that remained to them, the last link to the future. If they lost him too, they would have nothing to hold onto but each other, in their own eroding time.

'I don't know what we're doing in here,' Vincent smiled. 'I put out a snack for you in the kitchen. Coming?'

'Dad, sit down for a moment—'

'It's smoked salmon. Bit of watercress. Sliced Hovis—'

'I want to talk to you.'

'Fine. I'll go and load up a tray. We'll eat in here. Much better.'

'*Dad*—'

But Vincent was already out of the door. In the kitchen he ran into a little mystery. He remembered clearly having gone down there just after Rob had phoned to make the sandwiches. But there were no sandwiches to be found anywhere. He must have missed out that vital part of the operation. Still, not to worry, it wouldn't take long. He removed the salmon from the fridge. He used a pair of scissors to cut his way into the shrink-wrap and negotiated the thin slices of fish on to the plate with a cake knife. The cucumber was there all right, no problem; he sliced it very thin. But there was a moment's panic when he realised that the only packet of butter was in the freezer compartment. Rock hard. He thought of putting it in the oven to warm up. But then had a better idea. When he was rummaging in the back of the fridge, he had noticed a tub of the extra-light spread that Bubbles had used for years as part of her war against weight. He retrieved it now. There wasn't much more than a healthy smear of the stuff at the bottom of the packet. And checking the sell-by date he found it had passed by months ago, about the time when Bubbles' sudden and scary weight-loss had made a mockery of all those years of denying herself treats and even basic foods: bread and potatoes and sugar and meat and everything else that was nutritious, it sometimes seemed to Vincent. Now she couldn't keep the fat on if she tried. Now she could have indulged herself in all the forbidden things she adored – butter and chocolate and Marks & Spencer walnut cake and Häagen-Dazs Toffee Crème. Except that the treatment she was getting made her nauseous in the face of all but the blandest of foods.

Not worth thinking about that now. All said and done. Or almost all. Tomorrow would see the end of Bubbles' earthly story. Finito. In the meantime, life is for the living, harsh but true . . . There was just about enough of the spread left to give each sandwich a microscopic coating. As for the sell-by date – these vegetable oil things never really became obsolete, Vincent decided on the spot. Their shelf-life was pretty well infinite. So there was nothing in this particular tub of glop that could threaten the life of his oldest son, or his own of course.

Their oldest son. It was a year and a half after he had actually been transferred there that they discovered that Rob was working with a military intelligence unit in Northern Ireland. All that time their letters, addressed to him in Germany, had been sent on by the Army postal service and the reverse had happened with his replies. His letters had not given the least indication of this move. After they had found out the truth – an anonymous note through the letter-flap, hand-delivered one afternoon, neither of the Stablers were home at the time – they had gone back over Rob's letters. To find that he had never actually lied in them concerning his whereabouts. But they realised now that the chatty reports of his doings – the dances he had gone to, the trips with friends to the sea and to a nearby lake, a visit to hospital to get a boil lanced – were so unspecific, and so completely avoided place names that the activities could have taken place equally in Germany, Ireland, or New South Wales. The only piece of news in them that they could later construe as a deliberate deception was that he had been appointed a Physical Education Instructor. This information had surprised his parents at the time, for they could not remember him at school taking even the specta-torish interest in sports demonstrated by his younger broth-er, a passionate Charlton Athletic fan.

Nevertheless, when he was next on leave and spending a couple of days of it with his parents, Rob's story seemed to hold water absolutely. He was very convincing. There was much knowledgeable talk of circuit training and cross-country runs and bench-pressing weights and the individual merits or otherwise of various training shoes. Hilarious anecdotes too about recruits struggling and failing to com-plete the assault courses. Another weekend he brought home a PE colleague: Sergeant Jarious 'Jerry' Hurry, a towering black man of about thirty-five, who had been the division's light-heavyweight wrestling champion. Rob trea-ted him with a respect and affection that Vincent had to admit would have been called filial if an ideal world had existed where sons always looked up to and cherished their fathers. It certainly made him a little wistful to see Rob hanging on the sergeant's every word with such devotion. Still he wouldn't deny that Jerry was a very congenial guest, capturing Bubbles' heart completely, making her laugh, praising her cooking – which, in truth, hardly anybody else ever did, for it was not her greatest skill. By the end of the weekend he was calling her 'Mum'. (Vincent he called 'Vincent'.) There were tears in her eyes when she said goodbye to Jerry, and even Vincent was quite sorry to see him go, though he'd found the sergeant had taken up a great deal of room in his home, both physically and spiritually. So much so that when they heard some years later, via Rob, that Jarious Hurry had been killed, though of course Vincent had shared the shock and upset that Bubbles felt – that powerful, handsome, smiling man – his main thought was that there seemed to be quite a bit more free space and air on the planet suddenly.

(His next thought was to wonder, amazingly for the first time, whether or not Hurry and their son had been lovers. He had never shared his conjectures with Bubbles, yet it must have crossed her mind sometimes too that her boy might be gay. There was never any talk of women where Rob was concerned. Not ever . . . No, tell a lie, Bubbles did once ask him, in Vincent's presence, if he had a girlfriend. 'Army life, Mum,' he'd answered her with a shrug. 'Not conducive to that sort of thing.')

Not conducive. Anyway a couple of weeks after Sergeant Hurry's visit, the letter denouncing Rob, and explaining what he really did professionally and where he did it, fell through the flap and blew the whole PE thing to pieces. There could be no doubt that the letter – cheap white paper in an expensive cream envelope, ball-pointed capitals used throughout – was accurate: the evidence it gave, the knowledge it showed about Rob's life and family and career was so complete. After she had calmed down, Bubbles had sent a letter of her own, one of dignified protest, to her son. That he had lied to her, that he had introduced another into his parents' home to tell lies too (Vincent thought sometimes she was hurt almost as much by Sergeant Hurry's mendacity as by her son's). That he owed both his parents a full and honest explanation as soon as possible.

The first acknowledgement her letter got was within six hours of posting it when two uniformed policemen arrived at the front door showing a search warrant. They took away the 'Irish' letter, never returned it. There was no word from Rob, on any subject, for a couple of months, except for a postcard ostensibly from Germany – things were pretty good with him, how was everything at home? When he finally came to see them, Bubbles and Vincent's hurt at being deceived had been softened by the passing of time. Bubbles' main thought now was of the danger Rob must face every day of his life over there in savage Ulster. He assured her it wasn't so bad, not really, not all the time anyway – but his parents took it for granted that he was lying about that too. They accepted now that his deceit in the past had been all about trying to spare them the worry they now had to deal with. Although as Rob said at one point over this weekend, it wasn't ever that he *chose* to lie to them, he had orders to do so.

In any case from then on, Vincent knew, the background to all Bubbles' days and nights was an unspoken but heartfelt conviction that the phone would ring one day, one moment of that day, and she would be told by a voice she had never heard before – English or Irish – that her oldest son had just been murdered.

II

'What are you doing, Dad?'

Vincent looked up and found that he had to clear away a film of moisture from his eyes before he could focus on Rob, who he discovered at last to be standing in the doorway, watching him.

'I'd have thought it was fairly obvious.'

'You've been in here twenty minutes. Twenty-five more like.'

Vincent looked down at the knife in his hand, the smear of yellow spread upon the knife.

'Sorry, I – I was daydreaming, Rob.' Vincent tried a lighthearted smile. He guessed from the boy's subsequent expression that it had come out pretty ghastly. 'Though can you daydream at *night*? I don't know. Doesn't sound quite right, does it? But it wasn't the other kind of dreaming, you know. For I wasn't sleeping—'

'Dad, sit down. I'll finish this.'

'You'll need a tray.' Vincent lunged towards the corner of the room where the trays were kept. Then remembered Bubbles had reorganised the kitchen and he no longer had the faintest idea where anything was now. Ten days before her death she was rearranging her kitchen. Crazy. What was the point? But she wouldn't listen. Moving around so slowly. A tray at a time, a glass at a time. He could only watch, she wouldn't let him help.

'They're somewhere, Rob. Just let me think—'

'Relax. We don't need a tray. We'll have it in here. You lay the table.'

At least she had left the knives and forks in their old place. The plates were more of a problem, but he hunted them down at last. Meanwhile, Rob had performed his task with his familiar efficiency. The sandwiches mounted up on the plate beside the cutting board. A kettle was boiling as he was cutting. He broke off for just a moment to pour the hot water. Then lifted the teapot on to the table. Vincent had got the cups out from their new place on the bottom shelf of the main cupboard (made no sense, required stooping over or crouching down every time you needed a cup, he'd have to change it back).

'Teamwork, eh?' Vincent chuckled as he sat down to the feast.

'That's it.'

There was a silence as they both helped themselves to the sandwiches, started eating. Vincent discovered he was terrifically hungry. He felt as if he hadn't eaten for days. He bolted the first sandwich down in a few seconds. Reached for the next. That vanished too. Reached for one more.

'Slow down, Dad!'

Vincent nodded. Took time now to chew on the food in

his mouth. Swallowed. Waited. Rob poured him his tea. Vincent reached out for it, taking care not to snatch.

'I've been a bit worried about you, Dad.'

'No need. Really. I'm coping.'

'I've been specially worried since the phone call.'

'Which phone call was that?'

'I phoned you from Heathrow. It was only an hour or two ago. Don't you remember?'

'Of course I remember. Why wouldn't I remember? You said the plane was late, not to worry.'

'That's right. And you said you'd been talking to Jack Rolls.'

'Ah . . .'

The smile Vincent offered across the table then hovered uneasily, he knew, somewhere between the mischievous and the sheepish. Rob eyed him steadily, refusing to smile back.

'You shouldn't have said that, Dad. Should you?'

'Well, I know. Talking to Jack Rolls, my God! Bit far-fetched, eh?'

'It was daft. It's something that couldn't have happened.'

'I *know* . . . Because he died, didn't he?'

'That's it,' Rob said, after a pause. 'At least five years ago, wasn't it?'

'About this time of year,' Vincent said. 'Your mother and I practically buried him. At least hardly anyone else was at the funeral . . . I think I remember there was some old tramp in the back of the church, keeping out of the rain.'

'So were you joking?' Rob prompted him.

'About talking to Jack? I must have been. Lord, I could

hardly forget the poor old fool had kicked the bucket . . .
You weren't at the funeral, were you?'

Rob shook his head.

'But you remember Jack? And Audrey?'

'Course I do. They were always in the house in the old
days. "Uncle Jack" he wanted us to call him. Tim tried it, I
never could.' Rob grinned at the memory. Became serious.
'Then all at once he wasn't around any more. Nor Mrs Rolls.
We never knew what had happened.'

'Ah, you were still at home then? I wasn't clear.'

'Sure I was. Last year at school.' A pause, then the
question Vincent had been dreading for the past few seconds
– and actually, he remembered, had dreaded hearing from
one of the boys all those years ago too. 'What *did* happen,
Dad? Why weren't the Rollses around any more? Must have
been something. They were your best friends, weren't they?'

Vincent prepared to fudge and fib and generally throw
the blame on the dead. Not on Bubbles, of course, on Jack.
The man's drunkenness, very visible on the streets of the
constituency in his last sad years, would be helpful here. The
fellow had simply become impossible. Could not be allowed
in the house in the condition he was usually in. Not around
you boys. Something like this had been brewing in Vincent's
mind for years to be served up at such an occasion as this.

Why did Jack Rolls stop being our friend? Because he
was a drunk. It wasn't my fault.

But even as he prepared to deliver the lie, weariness
overcame Vincent, and he could not do it. It was not a
sudden conversion to honesty, he knew, but simply that the
effort of being a successful liar seemed all at once too

exhausting to contemplate. And after all what did it matter, what the hell did it matter now? Bubbles lay half a mile away in the back-room of a shop on the High Road; Jack Rolls was buried in a churchyard on the Isle of Dogs; Audrey was probably still somewhere in South Africa, whether dead or alive at this point he hadn't the faintest notion; and he was here, sitting with his son who was no son, and without a single intelligent idea in his head of what to do with the rest of his life. So what did any of it matter?

III

'What happened was that I slept with the wife.'

'Christ.' In the suntanned face the young man's piercing eyes flared in surprise. 'You slept with Audrey Rolls?'

Hearing it from his son's lips, the simple statement of fact seemed like the most damning of accusations. He was appalled at his own recklessness. He wished heartily that he could drag the revelation back into his mouth. Actually, in the strength of his desire, pictured for a moment the words, the letters streaming back inside him in reverse order –

Efiw eht htiw tpels I taht –

No good.

Was there any way back from here?

'We only did it once,' Vincent muttered now. He looked up and across the table. The eyes of a judge studying him. 'Honestly, Rob. We never did it again.'

He couldn't bear the grey-eyed scrutiny any more. He lowered his gaze again. It fell upon the remains of the meal.

The smoked-salmon sandwiches; Rob's favourite. He was aware that his own stomach was rumbling softly. It was not an unpleasant sensation – not when he had the means at hand to cure the condition. Without thinking, he reached out to the plate. Then stopped himself, ashamed that he could be even thinking of food. At such a time, such a dire time for Rob. It was – wasn't it? – what the Freudians would call a primeval moment. A sudden confrontation with the parents' sexuality, likely to cause horror and nausea in any normal child. It had certainly caused something like that in Vincent whenever he had contemplated his own parents' copulations.

His gloomy forebodings were interrupted then by a shout of laughter from across the table. He looked up in surprise. Rob had put his head back. Let loose another yell of mirth, and another. Vincent, at first not unhappy to see this reaction – it was better than what he had feared, it was better than seeing Rob storm out of the flat for instance, just like his brother had done years ago from another of his and Bubbles' homes – became restive as the laughter went on.

'All right,' he complained at last. And: 'Come on now.'

'I'm sorry, Dad.' Rob wiped his eyes. Seemed about to be overwhelmed again, but controlled himself. 'Sorry . . . "We only did it once"! How was that, Dad? Did you let the lady down? Mr Wood not at home?'

Vincent smiled tensely. 'I certainly did not let the lady down. As I remember, Audrey was most complimentary.'

'Were you a stud, Dad?'

'Rob, please. It wasn't a joke when it happened. It was – it was awful. When your mother found out . . .'

'Ah.' Rob sobered in the instant. 'Yes.' He nodded. 'How did she find out?'

'Audrey told her. Told her and Jack. Immediately after it happened. Why, I'll never know. Hatred, I suppose. For Jack . . . It was just dreadful. Poor Bubbles.'

'But how did it ever happen? Did you fancy Mrs Rolls?'

'Not a lot . . . Well, that's not true exactly. She was young, youngish, she still had a certain freshness. But I never would have if – it was the circumstances.'

'Where did it happen? . . . Not in our *house*?'

For the first time Rob looked pained.

'No. Of course not. I wouldn't have dreamed of it.'

'Mrs Rolls' house?'

'It was in Great Yarmouth.'

'What? . . . Why?'

'SDP conference. 1982.' Vincent took a breath. In for a penny, he supposed – it would all have to come out now. 'That is, conference ended up in Great Yarmouth. Started in Cardiff. Moved to Derby. Then on to Norfolk for the final sessions. It was the SDP's big idea. A *rolling conference*, moving around the country, showing off the Party. It had been a great success the first time they did it in '81. This time it wasn't really. The train taking the delegates to Great Yarmouth broke down on the way. Everybody thought that was a bad omen. They were right.'

'But what circumstances?'

'Pardon?'

'You said you never would have done it – except for the circumstances.'

'Yes . . .' Vincent was silent for a while. Then: 'Well, I was jealous, you see.'

'Of who?'

'Of your mother, naturally.'

'And who else?'

The silence went on much longer this time. Rob was about to prompt his father when:

'I was jealous of David Owen. Of the Leader himself. Although,' Vincent added pedantically, 'of course at this time he was not yet officially—'

'My God!' said Rob.

'Yes, it was completely ridiculous. Ridiculous of me . . .'

It was a relief to Vincent at least that he had to waste no time now explaining Dr Owen's place in the scheme of things. With another audience, even composed of another person who, like Rob, had reached his early thirties, it might not have been so. Much earlier than that and incomprehension would have been almost certainly total. He had the evidence of Bubbles' and now his own visits to schools and colleges to know that was true. And even if there existed a vague theoretical awareness, it was almost impossible to convey to an outsider the special qualities of the man himself. The bare details of his biography only hinted at them. Born in 1938 (same year as Russell Stabler, four years before Vincent), he had qualified as a medical doctor at St Thomas's, London (Jack Rolls had been at Bart's). Fought his first election as a Labour candidate in 1964 when he was working on the wards at St Thomas's, and was elected an MP in '66 at the age of twenty-seven (Bubbles had to wait until she was twenty-eight.) Once in the Commons, his rise was meteoric. Made a PPS on his first day in Parliament, he was Navy Minister at thirty, then Minister for Health, then number two at the Foreign Office, finally Foreign Secretary before he was forty.

On all this he had turned his back in 1981 to become a founder member of the SDP and, after the temporary aberration of the Jenkins' years, the Leader of the Party in '83. But more than the list of his offices and achievements there was a quality about him, and about the unique figure he cut in the politics of the day – a fascinating force of nature, driven by demons and angels both, a touch of Robespierre, a dash of Savonarola, trace of Napoleon, hint of Charlie Chaplin. Called 'Dr Death' by friends and detractors alike for his doom-and-gloom monologues and his cadaverous good looks. Regarded with suspicion by certain of his peers. Adored by the core of his followers (among whom Bubbles and Vincent were proud to be counted) long past the point when it was politic, or even sane, to do so. Generous, brusque, charismatic, paranoiac – a little. Master for a term of a Party that at its height was poised to take over the government of Great Britain, and in its death-throes was beaten into seventh place at a by-election behind the Monster Raving Loony Party. And all this within the space of nine short years.

But Rob needed no explanations. However much in his surly adolescence he might have wished to shut his ears and eyes to all of his parents' doings, in that house it was simply impossible to ignore politics, and above all impossible to ignore the Social Democratic Party. The name, the fame, the *point* of Dr Owen was as familiar to him then as, say, that of any member of Charlton Athletic's first team had been for his brother. On one memorable day the house had been graced by the Doctor's actual presence. Rob had behaved badly on that occasion; but since he always behaved badly his parents hadn't noticed much. Besides they were far too excited to care about anything but the honour that was being paid to them.

'My mum and David Owen? You sure about that, Dad?'

'No, no. Of course not. It was all in my head, but . . . you have to understand the situation.'

The situation. It had been a difficult conference. Three difficult conferences. While their visible aspect was of matiness, good fellowship, informed discussion, social drinking and lighthearted flirting, beneath all this showy camaraderie, darker themes rose early to the surface like swamp-gas. The rumours flew around. In Derby fistfights were reported to have broken out after-hours on the steps of one of the delegates' hotels. Also in that city it was said that graffiti alleging incipient betrayals of the Party by some of its own leaders had appeared on the conference hall's side walls. The words were hurriedly removed by the authorities, so the rumour went on, but enough people had already seen them by then and the evidence provided – names, dates, secret meetings with Liberal Party fixers – was said to be sufficiently detailed and precise to seem pretty convincing. The rancour in the streets spread back into the conference halls. Division among the high chiefs became apparent. At the Marina Centre in Great Yarmouth a speech from the floor on incomes policy appeared to criticise directly the Party's Leader – currently Roy Jenkins. The speaker happened to be Dr Owen's research assistant. Owen himself was seen to be vigorously applauding the speech from his place on the platform. The incident outraged not only Jenkins' close supporters. The Doctor was later made to apologise publicly. He was not entirely forgiven.

In this Manichaean world of trust and suspicion, friendship and malice, constant smiling and spiteful thinking, Vincent failed to flourish. On the other hand, Bubbles MP, as one of the Party's stars, was fêted and fawned on wherever she went. She sat on the platform (rather than having to push and shove for a place near the front of the audience which was Vincent's daily lot). She was always being drawn away for top-level policy meetings with other Party luminaries, or for photo opportunities, or to drink coffee or take wine or sit down to a meal with the business chiefs, media moguls and TV journalists that conference had attracted to whichever provincial town it happened currently to be in. Vincent, at first, was genuinely pleased at her success. But after a day or two, the attentions she was receiving from the Party faithful began to seem excessive to him. There was an almost hysterical tinge about it, about the palpable excitement that surrounded each of the Party's MPs when they appeared in public, as if – in spite of the confident prophecies that continually rolled down from the platform and were echoed back from the floor – not too deep-down the Party was preparing itself to lose a good proportion of its already scanty parliamentary representation. Everyone knew that a general election would have to be faced in the next year or so. The omens were not good. The opinion polls, which for many months had borne the Party aloft on wings of gold, had now turned inexorably south. The 'Falklands factor' was playing out its mischievous destiny. The economy was on the up-turn. Tories were strutting and bragging in a way they hadn't for years, and everyone knew that a significant part of the SDP's previous electoral support had come from disaffected Conservatives. It wasn't so much joy the delegates were showing in the frenzied worship of their MPs – it was the anguish of premature mourning.

But in any case certainly none of it was directed towards Vincent. Objectively he could see there was absolutely no reason why it should be. Bubbles was the elected Member; he wasn't. That was all. It wasn't personal, particularly. What made it hard though was the fact that both of them had believed – or Vincent *thought* they had believed – that what they had was not a solitary parliamentary career, but a partnership. Bubbles was the more visible component of that partnership, true. But like the iceberg, at least half of the whole lay invisible under the waves, and that half belonged to Vincent. In the hurrying world of Westminster, and again back in the constituency, everybody who cared to or needed to know, was aware how much Bubbles' career depended on him. Here, in these obscure little cities, in the fading October light, hardly anybody knew or, frankly, could care less if they did. Vincent was – nobody. A delegate. Dim husband to a lively, popular Member of Parliament: in Cardiff, Derby and Great Yarmouth that autumn it was all most people knew of him.

IV

'I can't say I see the attraction,' Rob said now.

'Now that's unfair. You must remember your mother started to put on all that weight only after the '82 conference—'

'I meant – where was the attraction for Mum? *Dr Death*? Not what you'd call a heartthrob exactly, was he?'

For a moment Vincent was speechless. This was worse than farting in church. Or admitting to young Tim on Charlton's Valley Ground terraces that one didn't give two hoots really about football. The Doctor not a heartthrob? With his piercing gaze? His aquiline countenance? His tall loose frame? His intelligence, his presence? As if the Brain of Britain had been revealed to have the looks of a movie star. Was it Bubbles who had said that? More likely they had read it in a profile and had nodded together over the aptness of the comment.

The way he had of brushing his forelock impatiently away from his commanding brow?

Then Vincent relaxed. He was letting things get out of proportion. As they often had got, he admitted now, when he and Bubbles were – if not intimates, then intimate acolytes of David Owen.

'You wouldn't have said that,' Vincent remarked peaceably, 'if you had known the Doctor then, in his prime.'

'I did know him then. Don't you remember? He came to the house? Looked like any other old geezer to me.'

Vincent would not rise to the bait a second time. 'Oh, Rob – anybody over thirty looked old to you back then. He was a very attractive man, I promise you. Even the men were aware of it. And as for the ladies . . .'

1982, end of conference. The farewell dance. Begun at some ridiculous hour in the afternoon to give the delegates a chance to break away early enough to catch their homeward-bound trains. Vincent was ready to go after the first half-hour. The indignities of conference, of the three conferences, all seemed compounded in the confines of this hotel's hot and dowdy little ballroom. Once again he was kept to the edges of the function, scrapping for breathing room against a mob of his fellow nobodies. Once again Bubbles was wafted into the heart of the affair. She rode a magic carpet above the heads of the throng; he was almost squeezed out of the back doors by it. Prowling on the edges of the crowd, between visits to the cash bar, he caught occasional glimpses of his wife. Chatting, laughing, listening intently, being listened to just as keenly. And dancing. Dancing, dancing, dancing. He could barely even hear the tiny orchestra that worked away on the distant stage. His wife was twirling and swaying to invisible music.

Inaudible music, he corrected himself, glancing down suspiciously at the glass in his hand. It was half-full. Half-empty. He went back to the bar, corrected that. Drank it down. Peered again across the heads of the crowd. She was dancing again. In the arms of David Owen again.

'Ready for another one?'

He wondered for a moment if by some trick of the sound waves he had just been permitted to eavesdrop briefly on his wife's conversation with the Doctor. But then, looking to his side, he saw that Audrey Rolls was beside him. She had two glasses of wine in her hand, was holding one out to him. He accepted. She was looking, he noted, very pretty this afternoon, in a somewhat flushed and sleepy-eyed fashion.

'What am I going to do with this one?' He held up the empty glass.

'Drop it,' Audrey advised.

And because he didn't give a damn at this point, and was so angry with things in general and his wife in particular, and because the idea of cutting up the feet of a few of his fellow delegates appealed to him suddenly very much, he did just that. Let go of the glass, heard it roll on the parquet floor for a bit and then, just as they were prudently moving away from the spot, heard it shatter into pieces. It was something that would normally have made him terribly ashamed to remember later, but by then he had far worse things to regret than broken glass.

'So you had it off with Mrs Rolls because you were jealous of—?'

'You've got to remember, I'd had a hell of a week. Feeling very resentful. Also I was a bit drunk. And I was at the very back of the crowd and it was easy to make a mistake, there was a resemblance, other people have commented on it—'

'Say again? What resemblance?'

'Well, it wasn't actually David Owen—'

'Oh, *Dad*!'

'Of course it wasn't. I mean, what would he have been doing at a silly little hop like that? A statesman like him? And he'd had a pretty foul time. Three bum conferences. He must have been wiped-out, probably heading back to Limehouse already. Or to the country home in Wiltshire . . . Anyway it was a chap called Malcolm Worthington. An-other MP. Looked a bit like Owen. Not nearly as good-looking though. That's who was dancing with Bubbles.'

'And there you were thinking—?'

'I said, I was miles away from them. And I was drinking. And – Audrey was egging me on . . .'

The two of them. Bubbles and 'Owen', dipping and gliding, gliding and dipping. The 'Doctor' leaned down from his splendid height to hear what she was saying, then straightened up and tossed his hair back with a shout of laughter. The band switched to rock'n'roll. Squealing with excitement, Bubbles was dragged between the 'Leader-in-Waiting's' long legs, tossed up in the air, flipped over so that her skirt sprayed out and revealed the tops of her thighs, a glimpse of panties. (Had Vincent imagined this?) Around them, in a circle, like elderly teenagers in a Fifties don't-knock-the-rock movie, senior delegates clapped and yelled and swayed with the beat. 'David Owen' rested his hand on Bubbles' bottom. That Vincent was certain of.

Even Audrey noticed the show after a bit, and she was definitely drunker even than Vincent.

'No need to guess who our Bubbles'll be taking home tonight.'

'Don't be ridiculous,' Vincent muttered. 'Bloody ridiculous!'

'It was ridiculous,' he said now, leaning on his elbows, staring at but no longer tempted by the remains of supper. 'I don't know what I was thinking of. Even if it had been the real Owen, nothing would have happened.'

'No heat between Mum and the Doctor?'

'Actually I don't think he ever even specially liked Bubbles. As a colleague, I think he found her a bit of a trial sometimes. She was always so optimistic, you know? And the worse things got for the Party, the more optimistic she became. You'd think that would be a good person to have around, but actually it can get so unrealistic it drives you crazy . . .'

Bubbles had been optimistic even *after* the electoral demolition the Party's candidate received from Lord Such and the Monster Raving Loonies at Bootle, Lancs in 1990. (Actually she had been optimistic, in a teary, this-can't-be-happening sort of way till the last week of her life.)

Long afterwards, Bubbles revealed that after her jive, which she had found embarrassing and exhausting, she had dumped Worthington, and had gone to look for Vincent so they could dance the last dance together. That would have been the slow romantic number before 'Goodnight Ladies'. But Vincent was nowhere to be found by now. Nor, though she made no connection at the time, was Audrey. Bubbles ended up, perplexed, at the bar where – no surprise – Jack Rolls was busy drowning his multitude of sorrows. Since her husband was absent, and since nobody else appeared to want to help the poor man get back to his hotel room, Bubbles volunteered for the job.

'You didn't take Mrs Rolls back to her room, did you? Oh Christ, Dad. Did Mum and Mr Rolls walk in on you?'

'Of course they didn't. This isn't a farce, Rob . . . Yes, I took Audrey back to the hotel—'

'That's a bit much, Dad. Your own room? *Mum's* room?'

'Not that one. We had another room, two floors down. I'd booked it so we could have somewhere for delegates to come and meet Bubbles, have a drink, chat. We were trying to raise your mother's profile in the Party. We thought we had a chance at the spokespersonship for Health and Social Security, and a bit of buttering up wouldn't do us any harm. But it was a flop; we could hardly get anybody to leave conference to come back to the room.'

'Except for Mrs Rolls?'

'Except for Audrey.'

Vincent sat slumped in his seat for a while. He heaved a great sigh at last. Shook his head.

'Well, there you are. It happened. Afterwards Audrey went back to her own room. Found Bubbles putting Jack to bed. I can't think she could have possibly imagined that Bubbles – Jack and Bubbles – no, it was impossible. But she took her opportunity. Blurted it all out about her and me. Jack was barely conscious. If Audrey'd told him the next day that he'd imagined all the stuff she'd said the night before, he might have believed her. But Bubbles was there too, and she heard the lot.'

While this was going on, Vincent was still in the rumpled bed Audrey had recently vacated. The sex had been good, surprisingly good. He had always thought Audrey's sexy public persona was only for show. But it had turned out not to be. The sleep he fell into soon after she left was deep and dreamless, trouble-free. He was woken from it by the bedside phone. The desk clerk. To tell him that on checking-out just now Mrs Stabler had positively refused to sign a credit card slip for the room Mr Stabler was currently in. Could he come down to the desk as soon as possible to straighten the matter out?

'Was she very hurt, Dad?'

'Terribly. We didn't speak to each other for – weeks, I don't know. Don't you remember that time? You were in the same house.'

Rob shook his head.

'I don't think we – excuse me for mentioning it – slept

with each other for a year, year and a half after. All through the 1983 campaign we were still hardly speaking, which made things a bit bloody difficult, I can tell you. And by then she had started to gain all that weight. Not that I cared really, but . . . Unhappiness. She was eating so much because she was so unhappy.' Vincent bowed his head. 'My fault.'

'Did she ever forgive you?'

'Oh, yes. At last she did. I can't remember exactly when it was. But one day – I don't know why, it was like magic – it just didn't matter any more. And then, I think, eventually it became a bit of a joke. I remember she said something funny about it not long before – you know, a few days ago.' Pause, then: 'The people who really suffered because of it were the Rollses. Not so much Audrey. She'd had it with Jack by then, whatever happened. She moved up to town soon after. And soon after that she met the South African and she was off. But it really destroyed Jack, I think.'

'He was pretty far gone by that time anyway, wasn't he?'

'Far gone. But not yet finished. I did him that favour . . . What a thing to do, Rob. And he had been kind to us. Bubbles really became an MP because of him. In '74 the seat was his for the asking, pretty much, and he stood down in her favour. And how did I repay him?'

Ten

I

I knew that Russell was worried about the state of things in the firm but hadn't realised he was contemplating splitting from Goldy entirely until we had our Sunday walk in the park. This was about three weeks after he had taken me home in the Jag for the first time. He and Anthea, with their two boys, had come over to my place for the afternoon. We talked a bit, then as promised they showed on my living-room wall colour slides from the holiday they'd taken in Switzerland back in August; and then, leaving Anthea to fix the tea, Russell and I and the boys set off for a walk.

We went as usual to nearby Bishop's Park, the long narrow stretch of grass, trees and statuary that runs alongside the river between Putney Bridge and the Fulham football club ground. I revisited the park a year or two ago and was amazed to find how many people were using it. Hundreds of them, walking and sunning themselves and watching the river and playing ball games. Yet in my recollections, from the early '70s, when I lived around the corner from it, the park always appears practically deserted, even on a warm summer weekend. But usually in my memory it is autumn, a damp grey afternoon, sodden leaves underfoot along the asphalt paths, a mist rising from the river and me, solitary, moving gloomily through it all. I used to go for a walk there almost every day. Scarcely ever passed anybody else, only a park keeper or a patrolling policeman, or an occasional lunatic muttering to himself on one of the battered wooden benches. On Saturday afternoons, when Fulham were playing at home, the park saw a sudden influx of fans going to and from the ground. Otherwise it remained almost spookily empty.

It was empty that afternoon when Russell and I started along the paths through the flower garden, the park's first feature after the entrance, with its surrounding statues of idealised naked forms, mostly female, some of them clutching nude children and babies. Each statue has, carved into the plinth, a single word title of a sentimental or inspirational character: 'Grief', 'Adoration', 'Protection' and so on. I noticed that there was fresh paint daubed upon 'Affection's' pudenda at the point where it emerged from the stone, and remembered that Fulham had had a home game the day before. The boys ran ahead of us. The afternoon was brisk, bright, early winter. Above us, as we entered the tree-lined avenue that runs by the river, the remaining leaves shook and shivered, making a brittle, silvery sound like tinsel crackling on a Christmas tree. I stopped noticing it in a while though, I was too engrossed by what Russell was telling me.

'Give up working for Goldy? But why? When you're doing so well?'

'I have to, Vince. He's losing it. We turn over – well, a hell of a lot of money every month, and I can't get him to concentrate any more. He'd rather talk about a fight Nick Gobelins got into with some spade in Lewisham High Street the other day. I tell him there's this opportunity coming up, there's that opportunity – won't *concentrate*. He says: "Come on, Russell, there's more to life than making money. Take it easy." Take it easy!' Russell shook his head. 'I'm thirty-four. I'm s'posed to take it easy?' He kicked a stone out of his path. 'And then this college-boy's bloody silly survey, whatever the fuck it is – I tell you, Vincent, I've had it.'

We had to break off then. The boys had found a frog up ahead and had brought it back to us. They wanted to know what to do with it. Would it be happiest if they threw it into the Thames? It seemed a very lethargic specimen, sitting motionless in the older boy's palm, only the rare flicker of an eyelid showing that it was still alive. There was a noisy argument about whether or not frogs hibernated in the winter. Russell was appealed to. He thought about it for a few moments and then gave his opinion that it was very likely, in which case it was probably kindest to put the animal back exactly where they had found it. The boys accepted the verdict without a murmur and ran off. Russell watched them go. He was frowning again, I guessed over his irritation with Goldy – but it was impossible to miss the pride and love for his sons that gleamed in his eyes.

'Will he let you go?'

'Goldy? Course he will. What's he gonna do?'

I was silent, though several unpleasant possibilities went through my mind. My brother seemed, as he sometimes could, to read my mind.

'He won't do anything like that. We've talked. Well, we're gonna talk when we get a chance. But he knows I got to move on, I'm sure he does.'

We had reached the playing fields. Russell had brought a soccer ball along and he tossed it down to the boys who began kicking it around.

'What'll you do then? Why, you'll be—'

'Unemployed' was the word that came to mind. But it seemed so absurd to apply it to somebody like Russell that I didn't finish the sentence. Nevertheless, as I still turned the notion over, unemployed it seemed was what Russell might well be. If only for the shortest of times. And I'm sorry to say that my first thought was that it would not look good in my parents' eyes. For them there were good jobs and not-so-good jobs, but worst of all was no job at all. They would try to be sympathetic, understanding – but they would be disappointed, no doubt of it. I even thought I could hear that grand old phrase ringing across their living-room again: 'Poor old Russell'.

Poor old Russell. I thought I might go and see my parents tomorrow. I only had a morning teaching session. I wouldn't of course break the news to them of Russell's suddenly altered prospects before he did. But I might hint a little here and there that things weren't looking all that rosy for him.

I'm slightly prouder of my second thought after I heard of my brother's predicament. Which was that perhaps it would be a solution to my own difficulties. I could – oh, how I wished I could – jack in my present unfruitful career, and climb aboard whatever venture Russell next set his talents to. Together, we could find something, an enterprise, an opportunity: the brothers Stabler, together at last. His business sense and my – well, his brains too and my – I was still trying to think of the unique quality I would bring to this fantasy partnership, when my brother spoke again.

'I'm thinking of going into politics.'

II

A pause. Above us, the breeze stirred among the leaves; they shivered and scintillated as if we had an audience up there that was tittering surreptitiously at the spectacle we made down here.

I'm thinking of going into politics. I had really heard that.

'Are you serious?'

'Sure I'm serious. You know I'm interested.'

I did know it, I realised suddenly, fatally. Russell was interested, and it was not some new craze or fantasy. I could remember him, back when we were boys, arguing politics bitterly with our Conservative (large C) father. The row over the Suez adventure in '56 had been monumental. And I knew too that as an adult he had kept up the old interest, was a Labour Party member, an active one too. Once I had rung him at his house. Anthea had answered the phone, said Russell wouldn't be back till much later, he was out 'knocking up' at a nearby council estate. The thought of Russell trudging up and down the floors of those twenty-storey behemoths, clutching a bunch of election leaflets, kept me diverted all evening. I knew he wouldn't be able to ride the lifts. In this particular estate, they were notoriously, perennially out of order. It was almost a national scandal how bad conditions were, there had been TV programmes about it.

(Was it, now I think about it, one of Goldy's early crea-
tions?)

So I knew, yes, that there was an interest, but I thought it
was just a detail, an interesting facet, in Russell's complex
personality – not a goddamn bloody looming career.

'But you can't go into politics,' I almost shouted.

'Why not?'

'Because—'

Because you're a criminal is what I wanted to say. That I
didn't was not because of any sudden cynical insight that
years of stealing, deceiving, and bending the rules were not a
bad preparation for the political life, but because my brother
had turned to me suddenly and was staring at me very hard,
and I knew I had to choose my next words carefully.

'Because of your background.'

'What background?'

What background! 'Well, you know . . .' I said feebly.

'My record's clean. Clean as yours is, I'll bet.'

'It can't be. Look what you've been *doing* for the past—'

'D'you think I'd ever let my name show up on anything
that wasn't one hundred per cent legitimate? Course I
wouldn't. It's standard practice. Put the money up, but make
sure you also paid off some other guy so he's ready to take the
fall. Goldy taught me that. I bet his record's clean as a whistle
too. Except maybe some GBH back in the early Forties.'

He turned away from me, was silent for a while. Then:
'Goldy knows some people along the river. Their MP's
gonna retire before the next general election. They're
looking for somebody. I've been to talk to them a few
times. They seem to like me. And it's a safe seat—'

I was looking at him now. His profile. The curve of his lips as he smiled suddenly at something one of his sons was doing. I had such an impression suddenly of – maturity. More than that. Of somebody shaking off the disguise of youth and indecision and rising to his place in the world, a world that I was never likely to see. Young Hal on the verge of leaving Falstaff behind. Sort of. I felt sick. I knew that it was over, the battle, the fight, he had won.

He turned to me again.

'What do you think, Vince? Me an MP?'

'I think you're too good for it,' I said, meaning it sincerely I believe.

He grinned at that.

'But would you really want it? All that speechmaking and . . . I don't know, kissing babies?'

'No, don't fancy that much. It's what's past all that, what it can get me to, that I want. Well,' he shrugged, 'you know me: I always liked . . . *organising*. Running things.' He smiled, embarrassed. 'Telling people what to do.'

'You want to be a – a minister, in the Cabinet, something like that?'

'One day – absolutely.'

'Lot of competition for that. Even to get noticed in the first place.'

'That's true. I know it'll be a long haul. But like I say – Goldy knows a few people. Pretty high up in the Party some of 'em. Should give me a start.'

The boys were calling to him now. He went down the grassy bank and joined in their game. I stood on the path and watched. I had no doubt that all would turn out just as he had said. Russell would be an MP. And then, in time, he would be – as he'd hinted he expected to be – a minister. Junior at first, even Russell would have to follow the conventions. But in time, no question, the great offices of state would fall to him in succession. Foreign Secretary Stabler. Chancellor Stabler. Prime Minister. Knowing then nothing at all of the incredibly tortuous and chancy nature of political careers, it seemed to me inevitable that all this would come about, just because my brother wanted it.

I could not bear to imagine the scenes of rejoicing in Beckenham/Penge when the news broke. All the news, every single rung up the ladder to the very top. And I the crashing disappointment, the murky mirror in which my brother's glory would shine with most lustre, the absolute antithesis of his own wonderful career. My only (pretty loathsome) hope as I stood and watched half my family kicking a ball about was that the other half would be dead someday reasonably soon. (My father certainly couldn't last much longer.) And in death our parents would take with them the worst of my disgrace.

The game ended at last. We turned for home, the boys running ahead as before. As we walked along, I wanted – and I didn't want – to raise again the topic of Russell's future prospects. To me, the whole business, so clear and inevitable a few minutes ago, had started to seem preposterous. A parliamentary seat, a *safe* seat, and the backing of a great party to be handed to a political neophyte on the simple word of a well-known local gangster? It just seemed impossible. There was bound to be immense competition for such a prize. Russell was surely – I hoped this so hard – walking in cloud-cuckoo land.

On the other hand, what did I know? Perhaps that was how things worked out there, in the great world of power and authority and influence, a world that for me was closing as fast as it seemed to be opening for my brother. In which case, to hear more of his plans and his great expectations would only be to turn the knife further in my gut.

Russell, in the end, as we were walking past the railings that separate the park from the grounds of Fulham Palace, solved my dilemma himself.

'This MP business,' he said. 'Remember I was saying something about it?'

Yes. *Yes.* But I didn't speak. Just nodded. Get it over with, I was thinking. Rub my nose in it, trample all over me, I concede, I've given up.

'There is one problem there,' Russell said slowly. 'And I really would appreciate your help on it, Vince.'

'Problem?' I said, and oh, the gleam of bitter hope that shone for me as I repeated that word.

'That's right,' my brother said. 'It's what you might call – woman trouble.'

Eleven

I

In the middle of the night Jack Rolls called again. Buried deep in the bedclothes, Vincent was able to ignore the first twenty rings, but the twenty-first brought him struggling across to the other side of the bed – Bubbles' side – to get to the table over there. He thought about looking for his glasses, but was too befuddled even to begin to try.

'Wha'?' he said into the phone.

'Stabler you idle bastard – every time I phone you, you're bloody sleeping!'

'Ja'?'

'Of course it's Jack. Who else would have the kindness to ring up a terminal pain in the arse like you?'

'Go away, Jack. Go and lie down somewhere. You're dead.'

'I know I'm dead. I was at the funeral, remember? And may I say that was a piss-poor show you put together for me.'

'Best we could do. I am sorry about the tramp in the back row though. We didn't have the heart to turn him out.'

'Actually that wasn't a tramp – or not only a tramp. Old friend of mine. Ted Stevens. You wouldn't know him. Used to be party agent for the constituency before all you carpetbaggers showed up. Had a few little setbacks at the end of the Sixties. Lost his home, wife, health, job. Spent quite a lot of time with Ted, my last few years on earth. I was glad to see him there in church. Otherwise? Pitiful. Ted apart, were there five people there, even that much? It was always my greatest fear that nobody would come to my service when I died. Such a judgement on the life you've lived when the church is almost empty. And you made my worst fear come true, Stabler. Thanks a lot.'

'It was all we could get to come to it, Jack. I'm sorry – if it's any comfort, I don't think I'm going to draw a much better crowd when it's my turn.'

'I'm sure you're right, and it isn't a comfort, thanks very much.'

'And poor Bubbles? Tomorrow? Today? Less even than you, I'm afraid. My fault entirely . . . We did our best for you, Jack. You were your own worst enemy though.'

'What does that mean?'

'Well, the last few years – you were a pretty sorry spectacle, knocking about town. Drunk. Messing yourself. In and out of the Emergency. People had given up on you. Why would they come to your funeral? Why would they even know about it?'

Jack was silent for a little while, and Vincent felt himself drifting back into blackness and peace. But then, he heard, wistfully: 'You couldn't have got word to the Labour Party people?'

'We did, Jack. I left a message for Bill Burrows. Telling him you had passed on. Asking him to spread the news.'

'Left a message for who?'

'Well, there you are, Jack. You have no idea, do you? You

were completely out of the loop. He was the constituency Labour chairman back then, when you died.'

'All right. You left a message for him. And?'

'I never heard a thing back.' He listened to Jack's grunt of anger. 'Look, Jack, face it – you dumped them. *We* dumped them. 1981? SDP? Remember all that? We tried to bury them back then. Why the hell should they come to our funerals now? I don't blame 'em.'

'I'll tell you who I *blame* for all that mess. I blame you. And your bloody wife.'

'I'm hanging up right now if you—'

'All right. I'll leave Bubbles out of it. It's just you then I blame, Stabler. You were the one who wanted to get us all out of the good old Labour Party—'

'Bullshit.'

'If you hadn't, who knows where Bubbles would have got to. By now she'd be a senior figure in government. Not right up there,' Jack acknowledged. 'Bit too old now for a really big job with the Blair people. But still a solid figure in the party. Respected. Influential. A figure of consequence. If only she hadn't listened to her bloody fool of a husband back in '81.'

'This is such bullshit,' Vincent rasped. He had to hurry on now, he had to say something. There was just enough truth in Jack's fantastic ramblings to make him uncomfortable. 'Bubbles was her own master. Mistress. I couldn't have talked her into anything she didn't want to get into. And also—' he cried out, his voice gaining strength after its previous slight uncertainty, 'if I might remind you, Jack, if anyone was totally sure that Bubbles had to get out of the Party, that she was bound to be deselected if she stayed, that it wasn't worth fighting Baz Jacobson and his lot, then that person was definitely *you*.'

Jack had the grace to fall silent then, presumably to reflect on the truth of Vincent's accusation. And it was the truth, they both knew it. It was Jack who had first mentioned the possibility of Bubbles bolting to the SDP. Vincent could actually place the location and timing of that historic and ultimately disastrous suggestion. April 2nd, 1981, around 9 p.m. – the place: Hanif Monnan's Tandoori Restaurant on the High Street. Vincent had had the chicken korma, Bubbles the lamb biriani garnished with an onion tarka. He couldn't remember what Jack ate. Or if Jack ate. Audrey probably had the vegetable thali. The food was good, portions were ample. Hanif, a leading Labour light in his ward, had been a staunch Bubbles supporter throughout the current disputes raging through the constituency. They had just come to the restaurant in fact from a steering committee meeting at which Baz and several of his supporters had made vicious, lying allegations against Bubbles. The mood at the table, in spite of the excellent food, and the discreetly sympathetic service – all the waiters were relatives of Hanif and had followed him into the Party, usually within days of their arriving in England – was therefore sombre. At last Jack had stirred in his seat, leaned forward to expel a breath of lager-reeking air over the Stablers sitting opposite.

'For God's sake, Bubs, if they're going to call you traitor anyway, then what can it hurt if you give David Owen a ring?'

'Baz Jacobson . . .' Jack was back again. 'There's an unpleasant blast from the past.'

'You heard about his honour?'

'What honour?'

'It's Sir Baz now.'

'Oh, bullshit. That's rubbish. The son-of-a-bitch used to call for the armed overthrow of the British state. Every fucking ward and constituency meeting. Fucking Jewboy!'

'Now, Jack, that just isn't necessary—'

'And every Saturday morning from his pitch in the High Street. *Sir* Baz? Unbelievable!'

'Times change, Jack.'

'So they fucking do. Look at me!'

'Baz reinvented himself in the late Eighties. Those motivational books and tapes aimed at business executives? Made him a fortune and got him on to all the right TV panels. Which led to his own show. *Baz Over Britain*. Remember? With the helicopter and the street interviews? Remember that one – or was it after your time? And then the Blair people brought him in to fine-tune their '97 campaign. He's working on the Millennium now, I believe. If that's a success, it'll be the House of Lords next for Baz is my guess.'

'What fools we were, Vincent. Why couldn't we have played it smart like Baz?'

'I wouldn't have wanted to be like Baz Jacobson, ever. He was an evil man. He made threats against Bubbles. Violent threats.'

'Well, so you always said. But you had no witnesses.'

'I was there. I heard him.'

'That's what I mean. No credible witnesses . . . We should have been like Baz. We should have raped, murdered, pillaged, kissed arse, done anything, anything to get to the top.'

'For Christ's sake. What top? Five minutes after Baz dies – and probably a long time before that – nobody's going to remember who the hell he was.'

'But they know him *now*. Because he's got a *visible* existence. You and me, my friend, we might as well never have lived.'

'Jack – he's a prat. Everybody despises him.'

'He's a visible prat, Vincent.'

II

This time when Jack fell silent Vincent found himself loath to let him go. Their conversation had reached such a mournful, regretful pitch that he did not think he could sleep again under such a burden. And sleep was what he needed now. Tomorrow – today – was likely to be sorrowful. And difficult, and stressful, and worse. For Bubbles' sake he didn't want to walk through it in a dozy fuddle. He wanted to be alert for her.

'Jack. Jack? Are you there?'

To his relief, there came at last an irritated grumble down the line. Vincent gripped the phone tighter.

'Look, you can waste your whole life regretting things—'

'I'm all right then,' Jack said. ''Cause I've got no more life to waste.'

'Well, I have. And I don't want to spend it thinking, you know, the road not taken. Or – ah, me, if only. All that crap—'

'Well, bully for you, Stabler. That's a great comfort to me. You know, Stabler,' Jack went on, in quite a conversational tone, 'that's exactly what I blame.'

Vincent suspected he had missed something, some vital link. Or possibly Jack had simply failed to provide one. That had been an old problem when talking with him, depending usually on just how far gone he was, how deep in his cups. The recent 'fucking Jewboy' remark was not a good sign. Jack had used to tend in that direction when he was extremely drunk.

'What do you blame, Jack?'

'Just what I said – *Stabler*. All the Stablers. If I'd never heard of you – well, I wouldn't be where I am right now.'

'Where would you be, Jack?'

'Don't play the innocent. I'm the trusting idiot who gave up the seat for you Stablers.'

'And Bubbles was always grateful. You know that.'

'I'm not just talking about her. The other one too.'

'Do you mean Russell?' said Vincent, after a pause.

'Russell Anthony frigging Stabler. That's who. I handed him that seat on a platter.'

'Actually it was never yours to hand to anybody. When it was Bubbles' turn, I grant you. But not then.'

'The hell it wasn't. I had the votes in '73, everything was going like clockwork. Week before the adoption meeting, I got a phone call from Ray Spruce – he took over from Ted Stevens. There's some big benefactor over in Blackheath, he says, who'll write off all our debts and buy back the freehold on the Party building in the High Street. But in return he wants his own man adopted. What did I think of that? Well, what could I think? What could I do? Course I had to step down. And that was the first Stabler who climbed to the top using my back to stand on.'

'I didn't know that, Jack. About Russell.'

'Well, now you do. Look what I gave up for your bloody family. Think I'd have been a falling-down drunk if I'd become an MP?'

'Some of them have been, Jack, I think.'

'Well, not me. I would have had – such respect for the job. For myself. Know what Trollope said about a seat in Parliament? Called it "the highest object of ambition to every educated Englishman". That's how I felt too.'

He was silent again, but Vincent could hear him breathing down the line, and felt no panic. When Jack spoke next, his voice seemed altered, it had lost its unattractive note of complaint.

'I'll tell you what though, when I first saw the bugger that was going to replace me, at the adoption meeting, I was pretty impressed, I must admit.'

'I can believe it, Jack.'

'And the few times after – same feeling. I never could get over having the seat taken from me, but I remember thinking more than once, well if it has to be anyone—'

'That's generous of you, Jack.'

'He had a quality, your brother, what was it? He was – impressive? No, there's another word.'

'Formidable.'

'That's it! He was formidable. I felt it always. Whenever I talked to him – and I wasn't nothing then, Vincent. I wasn't what I became. Well-respected general practitioner, that was me in '73. A leader in my field, almost. I'd just published an annotation in the *BMJ*. Nearly had something in *The Lancet*. People knew me then, Vincent, there was talk . . . but what I mean to say is: here was me, and there was this young fellow, what did they say he was? Car dealer, something like that? Something shady. Twenty years younger. And I was grateful he was talking to me! I was looking up to him. And it wasn't just me. He had the same effect on all that Labour shower. Even Baz Jacobson — eating out of his hand. Course this was the early Seventies and Baz wasn't yet the full-blown bastard that he became. Still in college, I think . . . But you know, I'd have put money on your brother being able to face down even the Baz of '81.'

'I would too.'

'How in hell did your mother bring two such different sons into the world?'

'It's always puzzled me, Jack.'

'Formidable — that's it. There was a man who would never get rattled, always stay calm whatever the pressure. You sensed that around him. Didn't you?'

Silence.

'Didn't you, Vincent?'

Pause.

Where are you, Vincent?

Have I lost you?

Twelve

I

'It's about Val,' my brother said. He appeared to review that
statement for a bit, and then: *'And it's about Anthea too.'* Still he
wasn't satisfied. *'More about her, really, maybe.'*

I slid a side-long glance at my brother's troubled face.
This was a rarity, I thought. Russell seemed to be in quite a
muddle.

'And about you too?' I suggested then.

My brother came to a stop. Stared at me.

'What do you mean by that?' he demanded. 'Have you
heard anything?'

'Of course I haven't. I'm just walking along in the park
and you start telling me—' I stopped, drew a breath. This
was getting out of hand. Mainly because Russell seemed to
be so uncharacteristically on edge. Suspicious. 'What do you
mean it's about Val?' I said, as we moved forward again.

Russell checked to see that the boys were far enough
ahead to be out of earshot, then he shrugged.

'Well, we – we've been having a – well, it just sort of . . .'

'Oh, Christ, no!'

'What's the matter? It happens. It's normal, isn't it?'

'I'm just – amazed.'

'I'm normal, aren't I? I'm like other guys.' We plodded
along for a few more steps. 'I'd have thought you'd have

noticed something. All those times I left you and Goldy talking and took her home in the Bentley? But you didn't?'

I shook my head. I wanted to ask why I was being given this information now. Not that it wasn't gripping stuff, but it seemed so contrary to my brother's usual close-lipped style to be blurting it out like this. True confessions. However, aware of the tension in the man beside me, and not wanting to ruffle him further, I managed only: 'Well, she's certainly very pretty.'

Russell cast a quick satirical glance my way.

'The reason I'm telling you now is – I'd like you to do me a favour.'

'Of course. What is it?'

'Like you talk to Anthea. Here it is,' Russell went on, when I found myself too surprised for the moment to say anything at all. 'She knows. She guessed something was up. I had to tell her. So now she wants a divorce. I offered to stop seeing Val. I told her I wasn't gonna be around Goldy's mob any more in any case. So I wouldn't be seeing her casually. And I wouldn't be seeing her any other way either. No good. She still wants a divorce. Right now. Grounds of adultery. She's already talked to a lawyer. *And I can't have that, Vincent.*'

I was following my brother's account so closely I became aware suddenly that my lips were moving as if in sympathy. When Russell stopped abruptly at this point, I felt myself still tumbling after him. I had to stop walking again, take some deep breaths. This was – amazing wasn't strong enough. It was unique. I had never seen into my brother's private world so deeply, never expected to, probably never wanted to.

Russell had come to a halt at the same time as I had. He was frowning down at his feet, his hands stuck in the pockets of his raincoat. The boys were somewhere else; neither of us was attending to them any more. Perverts might have seized them and be dragging them into the Gents'. We wouldn't have noticed.

'I would give her a divorce right now,' Russell said, 'if that's what she wanted. Perhaps it would be for the best. I can't say everything – well, it's not all that fabulous any more between us. And yet, I – I love her – sure, I do – but . . .' He shook his head. 'However, there's a reason why there can't be a divorce just now.'

'The boys,' I nodded.

'The boys . . .' Russell was silent for a few moments. 'I should have said the boys right off,' he said sadly then. 'But there's another reason too. The constituency.'

'What?'

'Lot of Irish down there.'

'Meaning what?'

'A lot of *Catholics*,' Russell explained patiently. 'Father Romney at St Luke's? I think he's OK, he'll go along with me, he won't oppose me anyway. But – a divorce? And the adoption meeting coming up?' He shrugged. 'It could sink me.'

I had it now. Russell wanted to avoid immediate divorce proceedings simply in order to secure his career prospects as an MP. It was as mundane, as shabby as that.

Russell!

At least he didn't try to avoid my gaze. He stared back boldly. His mouth was set in a dogged line.

'What can I do?' I said at last.

'I told you. Talk to Anthea. She would listen to you.'

'Why do you say that?'

'She respects you. Don't you know it? She's a snob that way. Books and stuff. And you with the degrees and the college job. Gets her all in a flutter.'

'I don't believe it.'

'Absolutely.' Russell was grinning confidently now. 'You're her type. I tell her – you picked the wrong brother, didn't you?'

'And what does she say?'

Russell shrugged.

'She doesn't think she did, does she?'

'Well, maybe not. But still – she respects you a lot. And you're family. She'd hear you out.'

'I'm to say she shouldn't get a divorce?'

'That's it.'

'Tell her you love her truly? Or that you'd rather she waited till the adoption meeting's over? Or should she hang on till after the election?'

'Tell her what you think best, I leave it to you.'

'Is this what you really want though? What about Val?'

'I've got to give her up.' I strained to hear him, the words came out so quiet. 'I know that. And I will. Yes, tell Anthea I said that, will you?'

The boys came running back then. They'd had some kind of an argument. They fought to grab on to Russell's free hand. Rob won. Tim, to show he didn't care, went and seized his uncle's hand. The 'old' brothers walked side by side, so close we were touching. The young brothers swung from our wrists and called insults to each other across our bodies. Chained like this, the four of us headed out of the park, back to where Anthea waited with the tea.

And then we got there, and she was hurrying about, laughing and talking, not seeming to have a care in the world, and shooing the boys into the lavatory to pee and to wash their hands, and then passing out the tea things to all of us, and I thought long after that this must have been the first time that – charged as I was now with this challenging mission to talk to her soon about some of the most intimate details of her life – I had ever really *looked* at my future wife. She was definitely rather pretty, I decided, and she had beautiful hazel eyes. I liked the way she wore her hair: long, and when she stooped it almost covered her face in a fine golden curtain. And even after two children, her figure was still slim and supple like a girl's.

II

And then after all it didn't happen; the talk with Anthea never took place. On the evening of that same day – and well into the following morning, I was given to understand later – there had been a mammoth discussion in which Russell had sorted things out with his wife. It had not been easy. The wound he had inflicted on her had gone very deep, and it was so hard for her to forgive him for what had happened. In an age of slippery morals and sexual carelessness, she was still operating on the codes of a former day, of the middle-class suburbs of the Fifties in which she had grown up. Whereas Russell – and I – had left all that pretty much behind us by now. Thus, though I had been hurt by my wife's several infidelities when we came to live in London, I did not think her behaviour particularly unnatural or freakish. It was just bad luck for me, and actually more of a reflection on my character than on hers. And I knew that Russell, while not in Matty MacBride's league, had certainly enjoyed other liaisons before his marriage and, from the hints he dropped around this time to me, probably during it too. There had been other Vals in fact (though I believe his feeling for her went much deeper than with any of the others – indeed, I know it for a fact).

'But that's not Anthea's style,' he observed when he was telling the story of that night of explanations and apologies. 'She's dead against all this screwing-around nowadays. She's always straight and true. Loyal. She can't see why everybody else can't be the same.'

We were in the Jag again. Driving down to Brighton this time. Russell had heard of a business opportunity, a restaurant for sale near the front. This would be a venture entirely on his own account. Goldy didn't even know about it. I had come along for the ride. Currently, as well as listening with interest to Russell's story, I was turning over in my mind whether this was or wasn't the chance I'd been looking for to say a dry-eyed farewell to academe, and to team up with my brother and start earning my living as – what? Chef? Sous-chef? Head waiter? None of these exactly appealed. I rather liked the thought of myself as a sort of *greeter*, though. Attired in a smart blue blazer with gold buttons and a pocket crest. Grey flannels. Club tie. The guy who meets you near the cash register, before you're all the way in: 'How nice to see you again, Lady Travers – Colonel – Nigel, you old scoundrel, your usual table?'

In the restaurant, I would be Russell's representative on earth, while he ascended to the heaven of Westminster. It would be something.

'I had to promise never to see Val again,' Russell reported.

'Are you going to do it?'

'I am,' Russell said. 'I can. Val's great – she's really great. We're like soul-mates in a way. But—' He shook his head firmly. 'Other things are more important.'

He meant his career, I supposed. Perhaps he meant his boys too. I hoped so. I said, 'And then there's Goldy, of course.'

'Say what?'

'Isn't Val his girl? Haven't you been sort of – well, betraying him?'

This shut Russell up. He was silent all through busy Lewes. On the other side of town he said, 'It isn't betraying him because he doesn't know a thing about it. We're careful, and he's not worried as long as Val's around, and he can look at her. Otherwise he doesn't, you know, bother her any more.'

'You mean he's impotent?'

Russell pursed his lips rather prudishly. 'I mean – he doesn't bother her. She says. He just likes to cop an eyeful or a feel every now and then, that's all.'

We drove a few more miles in silence, then Russell reached out to turn on the radio. But he seemed to hesitate when he got his hand on the knob. I glanced at him.

'I will say,' Russell nodded, 'that I was pretty impressed by my Anthea when we had that talk. She really rose to the occasion. She looks fucking marvellous when she's angry. Scorched me, that's for sure.' He grinned at me, looked back again through the windscreen. 'I was watching her, I thought: Christ, she's the best of the lot after all. And I'm married to her! And I was bloody glad of it, Vincent. It was like I'd come to my senses.'

The strains of something sweet and heart-rending filled the Jag's interior. Smokey Robinson, something like that. Russell hummed along. I brooded. We got to Brighton around lunchtime. The restaurant was a disaster. It had just been served a closing notice on account of its inadequate lavatory and ventilation facilities. It would need £10–15,000 straight off to put right before you even started with the redecorating. Russell walked out of the negotiation after ten minutes, I followed on his heels. We went to Wheeler's to eat fish-cakes and mushy peas.

III

Though my services were no longer needed to put my brother's marriage back on track, I found that my interest in Anthea had been piqued and I went more than a little out of my way over the next few months to find opportunities to be with her. Almost all of these, of course, were family events. Bonfire night. Christmas. Rob's birthday in early December. Anthea's own in January. And most weekends I found myself over at my brother's new house in the constituency. It was his,

Russell's constituency now. The adoption meeting had gone like clockwork. Unanimous, *nem.con.* Father Romney had been among the first to shake his hand. Russell's face beamed from the front page of the local paper, and also from that of the much larger circulation *South London Press*. And beside him in both snaps, smiling demurely and supportively, was the candidate's lovely wife.

But once in a while I contrived it so that I could be sure of being alone with Anthea. For instance, I went over in the middle of the day once to take her a couple of books from my own shelves. She had complained last time I'd been with the family that she hardly ever seemed to read modern books any more and she had been a great reader once. I had taken her a novel by Saul Bellow and the new biography of Zelda Fitzgerald. With both choices, I was aware, I had been pushing my case with her as the cultured, the erudite one of the family. Sensitive. Not because – the idea truly never entered my mind at the time – I had any intentions other than of trying to be friends with her, and to make up for the years in which I had virtually ignored her. The fact is for me she had been, well, just Anthea – Russell's girl, and then Russell's wife. I remembered their wedding day better than I could picture afterwards the face, the form, the dress of the bride. I had been best man, had made an indifferently received speech, had got drunk, had thrown up in the bushes – we were at a hotel outside Anthea's home town of Bromley, Kent. My own wife, having been prised out of the arms of the resident orchestra's bass player, had been persuaded to drive me back to Fulham. When she'd got me to the flat, she wanted to turn around and drive back to the reception. She may have done so as far as I was aware. I passed out on the bed and slept for fourteen hours. There were splotches and dribbles of red wine and something else all over the pillow when I awoke.

From such memories, God spare me, I recited piously, as on another afternoon I turned into the driveway of my brother's home. Anthea's little Fiat was standing there. No sign of the Jag. She opened the door. She had smuts all over her arms and face. She was surprised to see me. I had brought – it doesn't matter, I had brought my excuse. She let me in. She was cleaning a little room at the top of the stairs, which, she said, had remained grubby and unused since they'd moved in here. But it was fine, she was glad to see me, she could use a break. I sat at the kitchen table watching her as she moved about making coffee and standing tall to get some special biscuits down from the shelf. I got up to help her, but it was all right, she said, she could do it, you just sit down. I expect you're exhausted with all that studying, Anthea smiled at me. And teaching, I said. It's no joke. I bet it isn't, she said sympathetically, pouring my coffee.

We sat on either side of the table. Sipping our drinks, not really meeting each other's eyes.

'Vincent,' she said at last, 'I know Russell told you about – our bit of trouble.'

'Ah,' said I.

'He said you were going to come over and talk to me about it. He'd asked you to do that. I thought it was very sweet of you to try and help us.'

I tried to keep it light. 'What else is a brother-in-law for?'

'Well, you're a smashing brother-in-law.' She reached out and squeezed my free hand.

144

After that again we had trouble looking at each other.

'Everything's all right now then, is it?'

'Oh, it's wonderful. He's so sweet to me now. And—' A little smile flickered on her lips, 'I'm embarrassed to say it, but it really seems to have . . . livened things up between us.'

'I'm so glad,' said I, after a pause.

'Do you know what I mean?'

'Yes, I think I do.' I swallowed the last of the biscuit. 'And – uh – so how did you find the Zelda book?'

After Christmas we took the boys to the panto up in town. Russell had some last-minute constituency business and gave me his ticket. The boys were noisily upset at first to lose their father for the outing, but Anthea said, Look you're making Uncle Vincent so sad, he's crying, and I had to pretend to cry, and then – what the hell, I was the lovable uncle – sink to my knees in my misery. The boys came over to cheer me up. The six-year-old put his arms around my neck, the five-year-old covered my mouth and cheeks with sticky kisses. Anthea laughed and laughed and finally had to release me from her sons' embraces for their uncle was beginning to choke for real.

At the theatre, the boys sat between us. Anthea and I smiled at each other over their heads, and sometimes talked above them too, though with all the din of screaming children and yelling actors that was almost impossible. Also the boys naturally wanted us to give our full attention to the stage and would pull and push at us if we seemed to drift too far away from the trials and temptations of Mother Goose. On the tube home Rob sat in my lap, Tim slept in his mother's. She too was sleepy. Once or twice her head rested accidentally on my shoulder. Whenever it happened she sat up with a jerk after a few seconds, and smiled at me apologetically.

Meanwhile in these months, while Anthea and I were learning at last to be affectionate in-laws, Russell was embedding himself deeper into the fabric of the constituency and his local party. Even though the nomination had been practically bought for him by his patron, as in any eighteenth century rotten borough, still he was absolutely assiduous in cultivating the community. No school library was opened, no new adventure playground installed, no ethnic festival launched without Russell showing up, invited or not. The retiring member became quite paranoid.

'It's like having a bloody ghost trailing around after you. Or what's that thing—'

'Memento mori?' suggested Jack Rolls, who was his confidant at the time, and would later retail the story to Bubbles and me.

'That's it. *Russell Stabler*. My grinning skull!'

('Poor fellow,' gloomed Jack at this point when he told the tale, 'he hardly needed a memento mori. Died three months after he quit being an MP. Massive haemorrhage to the brain. Didn't even make the local paper. Or only on page seven.')

Nevertheless, Russell's omnipresence was generally noted and overwhelmingly applauded, and if there were a few rumours in circulation that there was something – well, a bit dodgy in the new candidate's background, it seemed to do him very little harm. Indeed in this run-down, working-class, riverside community, Russell's past and reputation as a bit of a villain probably had the reverse effect. They brought a satisfying whiff of the olden days, of the bully coves and excise dodgers of long ago whose blithe defiance of authority fulfilled the people's mutinous dreams. Those hard men with money to jingle, a girl to fondle, and always one step ahead of the hangman. For romantic militants like Baz Jacobson, it was the sort of thing that turned grudging acceptance of Russell's right to take the seat into something like hero-worship, and Baz was far from alone in this.

I went along to one of the party functions that were held towards the end of my brother's era – a May Day dance and tombola. Russell and Anthea were the guests of honour. The retiring member sat scowling darkly in a corner. Nobody went near him. Meanwhile, the Russell Stablers were the centre of an admiring crowd. I could hardly get near them. Anthea picked the chances in the tombola. She actually picked Russell's ticket for one of the prizes. A shout of affectionate laughter went up from the throng. Russell went forward to collect his prize, Anthea kissed him full on the mouth. I watched. Like everyone else's, my hands were beating together. With everyone else, I wore a delighted smile to see the popular candidate unbending like this. Russell gave away his prize – a bottle of whisky – to the party's oldest member: Lily Ann Tucker, suffragette, knew Keir Hardie, present tonight in her wheelchair. Everybody cheered.

IV

At the same time as he was involving himself in the new world of his constituency, Russell was trying to disentangle himself from the old one of Goldy's firm. From the bits and pieces of information I was able to pick up, this was proving by much the harder task. Goldy was not after all so relaxed about letting go his chief satrap and, I guessed, the only sharer of so many secrets of his empire. Russell really did know where the bodies were buried, and while Goldy was prepared to indulge his desire to become a representative of the people, and could no doubt see advantages for himself in his closest associate's achieving that position, he had never thought that this would involve Russell in a complete break with him. Moreover, Russell it seemed – again from what I was able to pick up on my now increasingly rare trips to Blackheath – had committed a cardinal sin in not explaining his future plans to Goldy until after the latter's political support had been secured and exploited. In fact not until a week after the adoption meeting. This was regarded in the firm as a serious error of judgement on Russell's part. Worse than a discourtesy, it was a deception. And worst of all, it served to make Goldy look foolish.

There were angry meetings behind closed doors. Goldy's shouts of wrath and hurt rang through the castle. The lesser gangsters stood around listening, sometimes grinning uneasily at each other, mostly wearing the scared expressions of children standing at the upstairs banisters hearing their parents arguing below. Val went in once, during an especially noisy broil, to try and smooth things over. Goldy ordered her out of the room. That evening, I came round to Russell's house by arrangement for supper. My brother sat in silence, hardly touching his food. Halfway through the meal he went upstairs. Anthea and I could hear him on the phone. His voice was warm and tender. We looked at each other. Both knew he was almost certainly talking to Val. I could see Anthea wanted to cry, but was refusing to give way. I helped her with the dishes, went home early. Russell didn't come down to see me off.

The squabble between the two chiefs had a baneful influence on the rest of the gang. Its intensity, above all the news that Russell was trying to get out, seemed clearly to mean that the firm's days were numbered. Instead of the prospect of an orderly succession from Goldy to Russell, there was nothing now to look forward to but the increasingly shaky rule of a fast-ageing man, a figure not of the 1970s, but a bit of a joke from the murky old world of spivs and diamond geezers and settling arguments with cut-throat razors at Brighton Races. It couldn't last; which meant that their employment would certainly be coming to an end and probably sooner rather than later. And however trivial the 'work' they did was, however mind-numbingly boring, it represented a steady income, and anyway was all they knew. Suddenly they were brought face to face with the prospect that they would at last have to fall in beside all those turnip-heads who had left school with them but then had got themselves into civilian jobs, had become motor mechanics, and furniture shifters, and bus drivers. The prospects were as stark and humiliating as that.

Of course these rifts and rows in the gang were of huge interest to Ivor Trasker and his people. In fact the survey was in the process of winding up when they broke out in earnest, but Ivor managed to get his sponsors to agree to a two week extension. Much of the material he gathered in that brief, turbulent period appears in his book in chapter 9, entitled 'Trouble in Thieves' Paradise'. For the average punter it makes lively reading and, of course, contains the satisfyingly morbid denouement to the whole story. When I first read it in *The New Barabbas* years later, my personal opinion was that it was just about the most flawed and superficial chapter in a study that is not short of examples of both failings.

Thirteen

I

The second-to-last thing he thought he remembered Jack Rolls saying to him in the night was 'I miss Audrey so much. Why did you have to fuck her?'

'I'm so sorry, Jack,' Vincent had said. 'It was the worst idea I ever had.'

The last thing he believed Jack said was 'I miss you too, Vincent. You prick.'

Vincent hoped he'd said, 'Likewise, Jack.' He meant to, but he wasn't sure he had. And then it was morning and Rob was knocking on the door. Vincent mumbled a groggy response and his son put his head round.

'I let you sleep as long as I could, Dad.'

'Wha' time is it?'

'Nine o'clock.'

'Christ.'

The funeral was at eleven. Vincent pushed back the bedclothes. He tried to heave himself up and off the bed. He tried two or three times until Rob took pity and came to help him. Vincent shook him off.

'I'm all right, just a bit dizzy.'

'I know.'

'Get away, Rob. I'm in my fifties, not my seventies. You can come round and do this for me twenty years from now.'

'I'm sure I will be. Now do you want breakfast?' Rob added, when Vincent had been got to sit upright, panting, on the edge of the bed. 'I went down to the petrol-station and got bread and eggs. You ought to keep stuff in the house, Dad.'

'I do keep stuff. I went to the supermarket—' When? *When*? 'Yesterday!' Vincent remembered triumphantly. 'I just didn't get – those particular things you mentioned. I would like,' he went on, as Rob seemed on the point of exiting, 'just toast, butter, maybe marmalade. I know I've got them down there. Somewhere. If your mother hadn't tidied the damn place I could tell you exactly where.'

But Rob was gone by now. Vincent took himself into the bathroom. Used the toilet, used the shower. Back to the bedroom where he put on underwear, a pair of grey flannel trousers, white shirt, the houndstooth sports jacket Bubbles had picked out for him at C&A's in Lewisham a couple of years ago. He looked all right so far, he decided, but a bit too sober. Bubbles would appreciate a colourful gesture. He found just the right tie hanging on the end of the clothes rail. It was yellow, mostly, it had a red rose on it, and bunches of purple grapes and other bunches of an unidentifiable fruit in a wicked shade of lime. It had arrived at the house a few months back from a catalogue retail outfit. They had opened the packet before they realised the name on the address was not theirs. Presumably a previous occupant. Vincent thought that, having discovered the mistake, they would of course post the packet back to the mail-order people. But Bubbles, who had laughed uproariously when the hideous thing had dropped out of its envelope, had been adamant they should keep it.

'Not our fault,' she kept insisting. '*They* made the mistake. Tough luck on them.'

Vincent went along with her decision, but he found it strange and even a bit shocking. It didn't seem like a Bubbles kind of thing to do at all. She had always been so scrupulously, pedantically honest. He was certain that this change was connected with her disease. Everything in her, even the moral and physical tidiness that was so much part of her personality, was crumbling and dying. Her speech was often vulgar now, filthy even. She told dirty stories – she had a repertoire of about ten, at least one of which she was bound to repeat every day. She didn't wash overmuch any more, a sour smell often rose from her in bed. In bed too she farted often and unconcernedly, and he'd hardly heard a peep out of her through all the other twenty-four years they were together. (Indeed, he guessed he must have outscored her in this category by a factor of ten.) He had to remind her to brush her teeth, cut her nails.

And now apparently she was not above swiping any bright item of clothing that caught her fancy. Like a magpie. So far the tendency was confined to whatever trifles and driftwood the tide, as it were, brought into her reach. But that might not last. For a few weeks he was especially watchful whenever they went shopping together, to see that she was not slipping anything from the shelves into her pockets and handbags. But he never saw anything (perhaps she was too quick for him), and a little while after that she hardly ever went out at all any more and the danger – arrest, trial, conviction, surely they wouldn't insist that she die in jail? – receded forever.

Anyway, thought Vincent, brightening, she would have laughed so hard to see this florid bit of silk around his neck on the day they were to incinerate her. Yes, she would have got quite a kick out of it. He left the room, humming, patting the tie in place. Halfway down the stairs, the thought of Rob's expression when he got his first eyeful of it sent Vincent scudding back upstairs. He tore the ridiculous thing from his throat and threw it into the back of the wardrobe. Grabbed the drabbest, least-memorable alternative that he could find. Was putting it on as he left the room.

II

Rob looked round from the stove. From the scents that had wafted across to Vincent when he opened the kitchen door it was apparent that his son had bought more than just eggs and bread this morning. Vincent smelled bacon, fried bread, a sausage. These were scents almost unknown to him nowadays. He had been, for years, a reasonably uncomplaining martyr to Bubbles' galloping vegetarianism, and then to all her special diets; the only time he'd been able to get a bit of genuine meat inside him had been on the outside, at a rare visit to a restaurant, or when they accepted an even rarer invitation to eat at someone else's house. In his own home he had eaten more bananas and semolina puddings over the past couple of years than he would ever care to remember. Now the juices in his stomach gurgled in response to the strong, unexpected odours. He hurried to his place at the table. Sat waiting expectantly.

'Bearing up, Dad?' Rob enquired as he brought the heaped plate to set before his father.

'Absolutely!' Vincent cried, striking home with his fork. There were baked beans too. Tomatoes. Fried mashed potatoes. 'This is grand, Rob. A fry-up! Good for you.'

Halfway through bolting down his third mouthful of grub, Vincent looked up to see Rob's eyes settled on him. There was nothing censorious or judgmental about his son's gaze – though perhaps there was something of both in the neat little stack of dry toast that was all that sat in front of *him*. As Vincent watched, Rob gave him a friendly smile, and put a piece of toast in his mouth. Vincent stared down at his own meal. It looked as if it had been the victim of a frenzied attack. The broken egg yolks were bleeding into the potatoes and turning the baked bean juice the colour of blood. He remembered a similar assault yesterday upon the pile of smoked-salmon sandwiches. It was getting ugly. He seemed to be turning into a Jack the Ripper of the kitchen.

He looked up then and across the table at his son.

'Are you bearing up, Rob?'

'Me? Sure. Why wouldn't I be?'

'It's your mother, Rob.'

Perhaps he had put a certain note of reproof in his voice then. He hadn't meant to, but perhaps he was doing a bit of paying-back. Rob's eyes narrowed, seemed to become more grey, more steely. He had his 'Red Indian' look now. Both Bubbles and Vincent had noted its rare appearance over the years. Thankfully it had never really been directed at them. One or two of his colleagues that he particularly despised; terrorists on either side of the Irish dispute; Ulster politicians and agitators – these were the people that brought out the Indian look. Until now, when Vincent seemed to have done it quite successfully.

'I know it's my mother,' Rob said.

He started smearing butter on a second piece of toast, using considerable downward pressure on the blade. The toast snapped into several pieces under his hand. Rob stared at them, and muttered angrily. An Indian, Vincent thought, with a knife in his hand, and losing his temper.

'Rob, I only meant,' he faltered, 'that it's OK – you don't have to be the soldier always – if you feel like letting go a bit—'

'Shut up, Dad. Eat your breakfast.'

'But I just—'

'This isn't a bloody talk show.'

A minute passed in total silence.

'I'm not hungry,' Vincent announced at last.

Rob got up, scooped away Vincent's plate. Took it to the sink, opened the door under it. A plastic garbage bag was meant to hang on the door's other side. Had hung there every other time Rob had visited. He shoved the still pretty full plate at it as he was opening the door.

'Rob, I think she—'

It was too late. The food hit the floor with some force, splattered in all directions. Including over Rob's shiny black funeral shoes.

'– moved it,' Vincent concluded a few seconds later. Rob stood, facing away from him, staring down at the mess. Vincent half rose from his chair. Rob still had his back to him. Vincent noticed that his son's broad shoulders seemed to be trembling. It occurred to him that Rob might be crying. Couldn't blame him. It was a hell of a mess. And then, of course, his mother . . .

'Are you all right?'

Oh God, he hoped Rob wasn't crying. For if he began it, Vincent would surely follow, and if he did he was uncertain whether he could ever stop.

'I'm fine.' Rob turned around. He was grinning quite broadly. Still, Vincent noted, he seemed to have something in his eyes, he needed to wipe them with the dishcloth. It was touch and go, Vincent reckoned. Rob stood there, shaking his head. Actually, he seemed mostly overwhelmed. At a loss. 'I knew she'd moved that bag,' he said at last, 'I've been using it all the time I was making breakfast. I don't know what – oh, shit . . . look at that.' He stared down at the mess. Then, wearily: 'Where did she move the mop to?'

'Sit down.' Vincent got up.

'I just want to—'

'I can do it. Sit down.'

He got the mop, and the dustpan and brush, started on the food. It was splayed out in all directions on the floor, and splashed all over the other cupboard doors too. He used the sponge on those.

'Look at my shoes,' Rob said.

'I'll do them too.'

'You don't know how to polish shoes, Dad.'

'Not like you do, you mean? Soldier boy. Don't be so sure. I was a cadet at school, you know. CCF.'

'You never told me that. Were you any good?'

'Hopeless. Had to leave. The uniform was so prickly it brought me out in a rash. But I learned how to polish boots.'

He had finished scraping up the food and mopping down the floor. He got down on his knees before Rob's chair. He started wiping the spattered shoes with a damp cloth. When he'd got the worst of the junk off them, he went back to the space under the sink. He ought to have some clear liquid polish in a jar stored in there, and a soft brush and a rag, and a toothbrush for the hard-to-reach places. Thank God, they were there, Bubbles hadn't touched them. He took them back to where Rob was sitting, crouched before him once more. When he looked up he was looking directly at the charcoal-grey cloth of his son's trouser-legs.

'I don't feel right, you down there,' Rob said.

'It's OK. I'm glad to do it. Anyway,' Vincent said, as he applied the polish with his fingertips, 'it may come in useful. I'm looking for something to do now, a profession, you know, a job? Maybe this is it.'

Rob was silent for a little while, then: 'Are you hard up?'

'No. I'm kidding. I'm not going to be a boot-black.' It felt though very peaceful and relaxing to be working thus. But would it be so to be doing it to a stranger's feet? Instead of – my beloved son in whom I am well pleased. The words flashed through Vincent's mind all unbidden. He blinked his eyes a couple of times to restore proper connections. Passed the rag this way and that to spread the polish. He felt his son's feet under the leather. On his knees like this, it seemed as good a place as any to say something he'd wanted to say for, oh, twenty-four years.

'Rob, I'm sorry. For what happened back then, all those years ago. I'm so sorry.' He heard a mumble of protest from above. He actually felt Rob's foot flinch a little away from his hand. 'I know this is not a bloody talk show,' Vincent went on fast, 'but I don't know how else to say it. And I'm saying it for your mother too. Mostly for her. I know we always meant to say something – she always meant to – but it was never the right time, and—'

Crouching, working, Vincent shook his head. He was stuck. He didn't know how to go on. Yet he and Bubbles had talked about this so many times, what they ought to say to the boys, what they would say when the moment arrived. Of course it always remained in the realm of hypothesis when it came to Tim. That conversation would never take place in this world, Bubbles had accepted that long ago. Perhaps even from that awful night, the last night she had ever set eyes on her younger son. Tim had just turned twenty-one; a week before he had graduated from Nottingham University; they had gone up to watch the ceremony and treat him to a congratulatory dinner afterwards. The explosion had seemed to come from nowhere, out of the blue, though of course the pressure must have been building up for years. Perhaps from the time when he was able to really understand what had happened in his family so long ago. Those dark, dark deeds. Anyway, when it came at last it was certainly spectacular. A terrible scene in the old house – not the old old house, the one in Eltham. Tim was drunk. He called Vincent a pervert, and his mother a pervert *and* a whore. He had tried to hit Vincent. They had struggled across the kitchen. A table had been broken. Bubbles had ordered her son out of the house. Melodrama, just like in a silent movie: Vincent had thought that even as he was picking himself up from the linoleum, more horrified and wretched than he had ever been in his life before. Only needed a piano playing violent chords to make it complete.

Tim was gone. Didn't come back, ever. Never took a phone call from them again, never answered their letters, never came to the door on the three occasions, spread over five years, when they had driven up to Coventry – they knew from Rob that he was teaching in a comprehensive in that city, they had his address – determined to make contact with him. The last time a dark-haired young woman had come to the door, asked them to go away. They didn't know whether she was Tim's wife, girlfriend, landlady: she wouldn't tell. Bubbles had stood outside the shut door, the drawn curtains, for an hour. Standing in the lamplight, under a thin Midlands drizzle, like a poor abandoned lover. Waiting in the rain for that little pipsqueak to show himself. Vincent had watched her from inside the car. He couldn't persuade her to join him. The boy never came out. Of course he might not have been there in the first place. His girlfriend/landlady had refused to say. In the end Bubbles had walked back to the car. Got in. They drove all the way back to London without exchanging a word.

III

A long-lost cause that one, then. But with Rob it had been possible to have the talk for years. Yet it had never happened.

'He knows,' Vincent had urged her. 'He can tell.'

'If I could just say—' She shook her head. 'Why can't I say it? Just to say that I'm sorry.'

'But he knows, I'm sure he does.'

She exacted a promise from Vincent that he would try his hardest to say for them both what she had not been able to on her own. It was not a deathbed promise. In fact it had happened a full six months before, on a 137 bus to Lavender Hill where Bubbles was booked to speak to an audience of Wandsworth borough cultural workers at the Arts Centre. (Title of her lecture: 'The SDP's Policy towards the Arts – a Vision Denied?') Nevertheless, Vincent had intended to honour the promise as if it was her dying wish.

'It must have been,' he went on now, hearing no response from above, 'awful for you boys.'

'It was confusing, I'll say that. Bit hard explaining it to the other kids at school.'

'Oh God, I never thought of that.'

Vincent looked up. Rob's eyes were flat, the grey of the pupils had deepened to a battleship shade. It wasn't the Indian look. It looked too remote and dispassionate for that. Vincent went back hurriedly to his son's left shoe. There was a bit of egg yolk crusting up around one of the lace-holes. He would use the toothbrush on it.

'You know, Rob, we would have done anything not to have hurt you two.'

(Except, it occurred to him on his knees, not do what they had done.)

Oh, the silence then from above. It went on and on. And yet what could he have expected? Congratulations on his honesty? Assurances that it was no problem, the whole thing had been forgotten, forgiven long ago? Had receded in Rob's memory to something the size of a peanut?

Well, yes, he realised, ashamed, he had rather expected something like that. At least he had expected a reasonably easy ride. We're making a mountain over a molehill that disappeared long ago, he had told Bubbles on the 137. But she had been wiser. She had known this was something that could not be stirred up without risk. Her courage had failed because she'd understood the danger involved; his had not because, as so often, essentially he hadn't a clue.

'Oh, Rob. You've got to forgive us. At least understand—'

'It's all right, Dad. We never really blamed you for it—'

'You shouldn't have blamed your mother either.'

'Why not? She was our mum. She shouldn't have done it.'

'Hundreds of women, thousands of women every year do what she did.'

'Not with their husband's brother. Our uncle. You.'

He could have said a few things in their defence. Above all he could have said that Russell had been mistaken when, in the park so long ago, he had smiled at the thought that Bubbles had originally picked the wrong brother. That though Vincent knew himself to be by a long way the lesser man, he was certain he had been the better one for her. That his personality had not oppressed her as Russell's had. That by his side she had been able to grow out of that dim, tea-making, mumsy shadow called Anthea into the great Bubbles herself: candidate, MP, personality. Able to trade blows – verbal and, on two occasions, the other kind – with the likes of Baz Jacobson. And with much more formidable men and women than him. She had told the temporary chairman of *Question Time* where to get off on one memorable occasion. She had refused to sit down during a speech in the Commons when a whole coven of Labour MPs had tried repeatedly to interrupt her and call her to order. Another time she had been so noisy and persistent in her own attempts to interrupt, that the Speaker had threatened to name her. And she had very nearly been SDP spokesperson for – for –

For a moment Vincent could not remember what it was she almost had been spokesperson for. He panicked. Shit. *Shite*. His fucking *memory* . . . It came to him. He relaxed. Health and Social Security. He rolled the words proudly around his mind. She had almost become that. And never would have done any of it if her marriage to Russell had lasted.

Yet it was pointless, he knew, to say this to Rob now. Because Rob had spoken the truth, the child's truth, the iron law that lies beyond all the adult evasions and excuses. She was their mum, and she shouldn't have done it.

IV

He finished the second shoe in silence. Got off his knees and stepped back to allow his son to inspect the work. Rob nodded.

'Very good. Almost perfect.'

'Almost?'

'Just a bit here—' Rob bent easily at the waist, took up the rag and rubbed a spot on the instep of his left shoe. '– and here . . .' He found another spot on his heel. 'There. Just right. Thanks, Dad.'

He got up. They were standing now a few feet apart, looking at each other. Vincent had the strongest desire suddenly to hit him. Which was a thing that he had never done in the old days. Then it had been a matter of principle. Now it was a matter of not wishing to commit suicide. He supposed Rob had the know-how to kill him before he'd be able to get one blow on target. Certainly to cripple him badly.

Rob smiled.

'Best get a move on, Dad. The cars are coming in twenty minutes. Spruce yourself up, eh? And you might want to use the toilet.'

Vincent suffered the indignity in silence. Found himself travelling obediently down the hallway to the downstairs loo. Inside, he opened his fly and took out his penis. Bubbles had always been generous and flattering in her attentions to what he knew – changing rooms, inadvertent sideways glances in public urinals, a horrifying visit with her ('Come on, Vincent, it'll be a laugh!') to male strippers' night at a club in Streatham – was a fairly average specimen. She had been kind about his whole, gradually thickening, slackening body over the years. He had not been so generous to her. Not for years. And yet he had been almost obsessed with her body once. And even when *that* stage passed, he had been pretty keen on it. But after that stage – then nothing much.

'It's because I got fat,' she'd say. 'I don't blame you.'

He had told her it wasn't so – but he knew it had been. He knew no way he could ignore his feelings about her changing body. And yet it seemed she had the secret where it concerned him. He'd asked her about it once, and she'd said, 'What does it matter what you look like?'

What does it matter what you look like? That still didn't make much sense to him.

He tucked himself away, zipped up his fly and washed his hands. Rob was waiting in the corridor with Vincent's overcoat in his hands. He helped Vincent on with it. It was a good coat, bought in the Harrods' Sale when there was still a little bit of money around. She had found it. The price, even with the Sale, was shocking. But it had been worth it, it had given them both a lot of pleasure.

He wrapped the fine cashmere around him now. Cashmere like Goldy used to wear, though his coat had been honey-gold and this one black as sorrow.

'Do you want to wait outside, Dad?'

'Might as well.'

Outside the leaves were deep on the pavement. They seemed almost as deep as the great heaps and drifts of the stuff that he remembered lying around at this time of year back in the days of his childhood. The council seemed to clear them up much faster these days. You could walk down most streets, even in full autumn, and there'd be hardly a leaf underfoot. He had a sharp sudden memory of himself plunging into those heaps, kicking them around with his Wellington boots. Leaves and the smell of smoke in the air. He'd be wearing shorts, he guessed, the omnipresent grey shorts that small boys wore in those days. The rims of the Wellington boots would chafe against his bare calves. Hurt like hell, and it was even worse later in the year when there was snow on the ground. But the leaves would rise and fly and scatter in all directions as he plunged into them.

My God, he thought then, he was having a clear memory

of a day that was over fifty years in the past. It was unbelievable. A man born in the nineteenth century, less than his own age now, might have looked at that boy kicking leaves around. And here they were on the brink of the twenty-first. He felt incredibly old suddenly. He had seen ages pass away. And he was burying his wife today. He was burning her. Oh, it was awful.

'Oh, Christ.'

'What's up, Dad?' Rob asked alertly.

'I forgot to pee.'

'What?'

'In the lav. I did everything else, but I just forgot to do that.'

Down the road, two large black cars came into view. One displayed a profusion of wreaths and cellophane packets of flowers upon its roof. The biggest wreath read simply 'MUM'. Rob's of course. His own was buried down there with the rest somewhere, he supposed. It wouldn't stand out. He had been rather mean in his purchase of a floral tribute. On the phone the tone of the florist's voice had turned a bit caustic when she'd discovered: (a) that he was the grieving widower, and (b) just how much cash he was prepared to part with.

But it was in a way Bubbles' real dying wish that he was honouring. Don't waste money on the funeral, she had told him. And he hadn't. It was how they had lived since the glory days had passed away, and most of the cash had gone with them. Being mean was exactly how, with practically zero income, they had kept themselves afloat in the past few years. It had given them satisfaction to be able to keep up their dignity on so little.

Rob turned back to him.

'Run upstairs. I'll tell 'em to wait.'

'No, Rob. I'll be all right. I can hold on.'

'You can't hold on for that long.'

'There'll be one at the crematorium. I'll go there if I have to.'

The cars came to a halt beside them. A fellow in a black suit got out of the front one.

'Stabler?'

'That's us,' Rob said.

He was trying not to look in the rear of the front car. The hearse. Vincent had no problems doing it. There it was. Bubbles' coffin. Flowers on that too.

'Such a lot of flowers,' he said. 'I didn't think we knew so many people.'

The undertaker's man showed them to the second car, opened the door for them. They sat on either side of the rear seat, what seemed like acres of space between them. They moved off. Vincent watched the preceding car for a while then, as they entered the traffic stream, he looked out of his side-window. Little shops, cafés, big petrol stations, Friday Night Is Bingo Night, fish and chips, a police station built in 1910 and looking in better shape than the school further along the road which had been opened in 1975 – he had time to read this on the plaque outside the gate, the traffic was crawling along – by the then Secretary of State for Education. Who was that? Vincent tried to remember. He ought to be able to, it was during their time. Couldn't though. The car speeded up a little. He went back to his sightseeing. A squat glass and steel box looking for tenants at £50 per square foot, bars, clubs, a couple of old pubs with new and foolish names, a video-game arcade, a drive-thru Burger King, Dixon's, a charity shop, another petrol-station, a church, a broken signboard in front of it: 'Jesus Christ – Not Just For Christmas', a man in a ragged University of Michigan parka selling the *Big Issue* outside an Iceland store.

South London. What a bloody awful place to spend a life in, Vincent thought. Sarf sodding London. Good enough for him, but she should have had better. Wherever lively, important, involved people congregated, that's where she had belonged. Decision-makers. He really thought that in her prime she could have gone anywhere, dominated any scene. Anywhere in the world. But the years had gone by and they had never really moved far from the places where both had been born and grown up. They had not even claimed their share of the latterly-fashionable areas that lay along the south bank of the Thames in Battersea, Wandsworth, Docklands. It was down here, far from the river, in this interminable maze of seedy streets and low buildings and lower expectations that they had made their homes. Those few years when she had flourished at Westminster, and he had flourished with her, in the tail of her comet, seemed to him now like a total aberration. They had been living off that time ever since, like two cockroaches subsisting for months on a single human hair.

And surely the fault for that had been mainly his. Not that he hadn't been ambitious himself, in a way – but that he had grown timid, and unadventurous, and slothful. Increasingly he had been a negative influence. So she had let slip by the chances that had come up over the years – there had been talk once of her going to work for the Council of Europe in Strasbourg, for instance – and, with him, had subsided into an unthreatening rut: the lectures, the shopping, the TV every night, the memories. Their obscurity, accepted by her but really contrived by him. Fifteen years of it. His fault. That her dying had received almost no public notice was a verdict much more on him, than on her.

And yet – and yet – Vincent's hands bunched into fists as he strained to comprehend. And yet their time together had not been without accomplishment. He had not always been a coward, and she had been – almost dazzling once. All those things that ran through his mind so often – the victories at the polls, the good things that were achieved for the constituents, the informed (credit Vincent) and effective speeches in the House, a half-dozen successful appearances on *Question Time*, standing up to Baz Jacobson and his red hordes in the constituency, triumph and disaster – she had done them all. And he had been behind her all the way. If he had held her back ever since – and even maybe a bit back then, during the glory years – then he had held her *up* too. She depended on him. She had said so often. She had said that she could not imagine life without him.

They had done things together once. Things that mattered. They had lived. They certainly had.

'What did you say, Dad?' Rob asked.

'I didn't say anything – did I say something?'

Rob was observing his bunched fists. He reached out and took hold of one of Vincent's hands.

'Not to worry, Dad,' he said.

'OK.' Vincent sighed and said again, 'OK.'

He looked out of the window then, without animosity this time. South London. Ah well. Not one of the least favourable spots on earth after all. There were plenty worse, probably. Except for a few years back in the Forties, it had not been a scene of warfare in their time, nor of plagues, nor famine, and of riots there had only been a couple of the serious variety, and those not very close to them. And at least, as Bubbles always said, in South London one never had to dress up to go outside.

'Are we coming back in this car, Rob?'

'No, Dad. Friend of mine's leaving his motor at the crematorium. I'll drive us back.'

'Army friend?'

'School friend. Remember Andy Laycock?'

'Not really.'

'Here we are, Dad.'

They passed under the crematorium arch. Peering ahead, past the car that carried Bubbles, Vincent saw a great crowd of people waiting around the entrance to the chapel.

'They must have booked another service at the same time,' he grumbled. 'That's not right.'

'Actually, I think those people are for Mum.'

'Can't be.' Vincent shook his head. 'I put them all off. Didn't I tell you?'

'Yes, you did,' Rob said gently. 'But I didn't think it was such a good idea. So I phoned a few people – and got them each to phone a few others and so on and – well, here they are.'

Vincent became aware that all this time he had been

holding on to Rob's hand. He let it go now. Stared at the young man, as the car glided to a halt.

'You did that?'

'I thought I ought to, Dad . . . I'm sorry but – you know, it's not only us that wants to say goodbye to her.'

A moment, then Vincent looked out of the side-window at the crowd. He thought he recognised a few faces. The limo driver was opening the door, stepping back to allow Vincent out. Rob put his hand flat against Vincent's back to steady him.

Vincent cried out.

'Rob!'

'What's that, Dad?'

'I think I see your father.'

Fourteen

I

The weather that day was very fine. Easter Sunday, and though it came early that year for once the celebration of the risen God had not had to take place to the accompaniment of stormy skies and Arctic winds. Arriving at Goldy's for the regular brunch, I found a full castle. Almost every element in the well-populated and heterogeneous universe – 'the circus' as Russell was accustomed to call it now – that Goldy had constructed, or let fall into place around him in the past few months, was represented: gangsters, girlfriends, researchers, researchers' wives, business associates, political cronies, Ivor Trasker, myself. Everybody present and accounted for.

And Russell and Val were there too. The sheer fact of it didn't surprise me. Anthea's prohibition on her husband's ever seeing 'that girl' again was never meant, I knew, to be taken literally. Since Val was a fixture at Goldy's, part of the household, and Russell had to go there sometimes to conduct his business, it was inevitable that they would meet. Anthea must have known that. But I understood that the spirit of the conditions she had insisted upon if the marriage was to be saved, and which Russell had accepted, was that he and Val would no longer share any kind of intimacy in thought or word or deed. They were to be no longer an 'item'. They were certainly not to conduct themselves in such a manner as I found them, shortly after my arrival, when I went to hang up my coat in a little cloakroom off the main hallway, in each other's arms, kissing, her hands in his hair, one of his slipped under the waistband of her skirt and, invisibly but manifestly, stroking her behind.

Russell looked up from the embrace, his gaze settled on me, he smiled. It occurred to me that he was taking a shocking risk. The door was unlocked. Anybody could have walked in. It was pure luck it happened to be only me. And the next thing that occurred to me was that if a cautious man like Russell was going to be so careless – then it was because he was beyond caring. He had gone over the edge. Where his feeling for Val was concerned, he didn't give a toss about hiding it any more.

'Oh,' I said. And: 'Sorry, I'm – I'm looking for Goldy.'

Hearing me, Val turned her head. She too smiled to see me. Her eyes in the dim light seemed milky with rapture. Russell's hidden hand was still kneading her perfect bottom. I was embarrassed to find that, just imagining that tremendous contact, I was getting a little excited myself.

'Sorry,' I said again, backing out.

'Think Goldy's in the conservatory,' Russell called after me in a lazy, uninterested voice.

I went to find out. Down the rest of the hallway, through the double-lounge where two long tables had been set up to accommodate both the regular attendees at Sunday brunch and the extra guests that Easter and the fine weather had brought out, past the potted bay trees that guarded on either side the narrow entrance to the conservatory. Inside, I found Goldy in close conference with Johnny Blake. I thought I would join them, or at least sit somewhere where I could attract Goldy's attention when there was a break in the discussion. I felt strongly a need to speak to him. I had not been at the castle, nor seen him anywhere else, for nearly a month, the longest gap in our acquaintance since it had begun on that November night in Fulham a year and a half ago. I missed him.

Johnny Blake was crying. Great rolling tears coursing down his face. I saw them just as I was lowering myself on to a sofa. At the same moment Goldy cast a quick, warning glance at me. I straightened up, muttered an apology, backed out of the room. I hung about near the bay trees for a bit, then having nothing else to do, wandered over to the nearest table and sat down. Somebody passed me a cup of coffee. Toast appeared. Scrambled eggs. A dish of smoked-mackerel. I was sitting between the chairman of the planning committee of a London borough situated way to the west and a man I'd been introduced to on a previous occasion in this house as the manager of a glam-rock band, currently popular. On the other side of the table two of the researchers were wolfing down food as if they hadn't eaten since the preceding Sunday. Which probably wasn't far from the case.

Nobody seemed keen to talk to me, so I ate in silence, and thought about the surprising scene I had encountered just then in the conservatory. But perhaps it wasn't all that surprising. I supposed that if anybody in Goldy's entourage was going to be discovered crying his eyes out on a lovely Sunday afternoon, it was likely to be Johnny Blake. I knew him to be a young man of particularly intense emotions, usually those of rage. We all knew to stay clear when Johnny Blake was in a state.

I took a second cup of coffee. Though the lovely weather

had raised my spirits for a time, I felt very jangled and bothered this day. Actually I felt like crying too. My life – my God. Everything in it seemed to be spiralling downwards to some appalling conclusion. Things at work were very bad, and the worse they got the less I felt able to show up to try to deal with them. I had missed all my classes for a week. Ten days, I corrected myself. I had not seen my students individually since the beginning of term. Justifiably they were angry, were complaining to my superiors. I believed a petition was circulating, calling for my dismissal if the situation did not improve. I think I would have signed it if it had come my way.

Such personal life as I could be said to have was certainly no improvement. I had received a letter the day before from my wife. It contained a number of Polaroids. This in response to a plea I had sent her to forward some recent snaps of our baby. (No longer a baby though, I had to keep telling myself, almost two years old.) The Polaroids showed her all right. Smiling joyously into the California sunshine, she was sitting on the lap of a man who I had never seen before. A scraggly-bearded man, thin to the point of emaciation. I was able to appreciate this as he was stark naked. So was my wife, who sat beside him, her hand resting on his arm, her face pushed against his shoulder. My sweet daughter of course was naked too. Under her little bare bum, the man's circumcised tool hung meatily between his legs. A brief note accompanied the pictures:

The babe is really responding to Ziggo. He's a great guy, a true father-figure, and has totally sworn to keep the drugs out of

*her sight and definitely not to shoot up in her presence. So far
he's kept his promise. Cross-fingers!*

I didn't, after the initial panic, believe that my daughter was
facing any real risk. Whatever the troubles between us, I
knew Matty to be a good mother. I knew she was 'teasing'
me; she might even have kidded herself that I would get a
laugh out of both photo and note. Who the hell 'Ziggo' was I
didn't know, but, if he was the junkie that his painfully
skinny body suggested, then I was pretty certain he'd go
home minus those drooping balls, caught by the camera in
such refulgent detail, if he ever dared bring his works into
her house. Actually I wouldn't have put it past her to have
hired Ziggo to pose for these pictures. All in the good cause
of achieving revenge for my and England's having disappointed her so cruelly.

It was not the least of the sorrows these pictures brought
me that they had been so cunningly posed that I would not
be able to scissor out of them entirely the corrupt, unwanted
adult flesh so that I might preserve alone and pure the vision
of my golden child. I had the choice therefore of keeping a
lot of Ziggo, and Matty MacBride too, or throwing away the
whole lot. I still hadn't made up my mind.

II

I felt a tap on my shoulder then, looked up. Nick Gobelins.
He jerked a thumb towards the conservatory.

'Goldy wants a word.'

I found him alone this time. He was stooped over a row of pots, using a little watering can on them. He straightened up when I came in and held out his hand.

'Hello, stranger,' he said.

When we had finished shaking hands, he put the can carefully away, then lowered himself on the sofa. He patted the seat next to him, so recently occupied by Johnny Blake.

'Is he OK?' I asked as I sat.

'Who? Oh, Johnny? Yeah, sure, he was just a bit upset. His father's gone home to Ireland to die, that's all . . . What?'

This, I suppose, addressed to whatever expression had just appeared on my face.

'It's just – I hadn't exactly imagined Johnny Blake with parents.'

Goldy gave me a strange look. I hurried to make amends.

'I mean – I suppose they were close, him and his dad?'

'No, they weren't. And now they never will be. That's what's upset him. He's a very sensitive boy.'

Goldy dismissed the subject with a regretful little wave of his hand. He contemplated me in silence for a full half-minute. I was glad to find that his expression as he did this was thoughtful rather than hostile.

'Where have you been, Vincent?' he asked at last.

'Ah, well—'

'You haven't been here, that's for sure . . . Busy at college?'

I tried to agree with that but, in view of the cold truth of the matter, the effort was beyond me. I shook my head.

'I didn't think you'd want me around. I know – I know

there's been a bit of trouble between you and Russell. I thought I'd better – Ah!'

I stopped, not before giving quite a yelp of pain. Goldy had reached out suddenly and seized my arm, digging his fingers deep into my flesh.

'Now that's a load of bollocks,' he said.

He still had not released me, and it was still hurting enough to make me gasp. I wondered at so much grip being exerted by a man who though, as always, looked to be in good shape for his age, was still a full thirty years older than me.

'Don't you know it's bollocks?'

'I suppose so,' I groaned, and he let go of me. Still he kept studying my face. His expression had returned to the benevolent regard with which he usually favoured me. But he was shaking his head. Then that stopped and he appeared to be thinking something over. At last he nodded.

'Let me tell you about these two brothers I knew once. Twin brothers. This was just after the war, over in Catford. Tony and Alfie Kostafides. So Tony and me had a bit of a barney. He got out of his depth on something – I lost a lot of money because of it. Lot of money for those days.' His eyes gleamed reminiscently. 'Hundred and fifty pounds I think it was.'

'Go on, Goldy.'

'So – I had to have him hurt. It was out of my hands, it gotta be done. For the example. He was in hospital a few months. I think he emigrated afterwards. Australia maybe? He couldn't face his old mates in Catford, not the way he looked now. He'd been a handsome fella, you see.'

'Are you going to have Russell hurt?'

'Not the point of the story. The point is – my friendship with brother Alf stayed just as it was. It did not change one bleeding jot. Because Alfie understood – and I understood – and even *Tony* understood – that things that happen from a purely business point of view are nobody's concern except the people directly involved. Had I gone after Tony for a personal reason, then of course Alfie would have felt bound to get into it. But I didn't, so he didn't. We stayed the best of friends. In fact,' Goldy nodded, 'I think he might be here this afternoon. I'll introduce you if I see him.'

'Where's Tony Kostafides?'

'Dead, I think. Or still in Australia. It was a long time ago these things happened, Vincent. Over the years, people just disappear . . . Now – does this make you feel any better?'

'Um.'

'Whatever aggro there is between Russell and me – and it's gonna get sorted out, believe me – I don't want you thinking you have to take sides. It's only business.'

I had a sudden flash of Russell, a couple of score yards away, in the arms of Goldy's girlfriend.

'I understand,' I said.

'Good.' He took and shook my hand again. 'It's terrific to see you, Vincent. Are you gonna stay long?'

'I've got no other plans.'

'Going up to the fair?'

(Such a simple, innocuous question. It should have been accompanied by croaking ravens and wailing women and any other harbingers of doom that were handy in 'Heath's Edge' that sunny day.)

'What fair?' I asked.

'Up Blackheath. I think some of the boys are going to it later. You should go. You look like you need cheering up.'

After that we talked for what, in my memory, seems like ages. Perhaps it was only half- or three-quarters-of-an-hour. People kept appearing in the conservatory doorway wanting his attention. He waved them away every time. I felt so flattered. I told him everything that was going on, going wrong in my life. I don't remember if he had any suggestions as to how I could fix any of them. He probably recognised, as I was to soon enough, that they were beyond fixing. The only recourse left to me was to let go of them all. Which I was to do over the next few weeks and months. Leave my job. Give up trying to satisfy my parents' exorbitant dreams for my 'success'. Cut myself off finally from the unsalvable pain of my child's absence, which meant snapping the bond with my daughter. A thing so dreadful that even now I can't write of it without feeling my stomach knot up. But it had to be done.

At last Goldy was visited by someone who had the authority to take his attention away from me. He nodded at whoever now stood in the doorway, and turned back to me with an expression which said it was probably about time for me to wrap up my monologue. I looked to see who it was that had this power. Of course it was Russell. Standing there, leaning against the door frame, watching us. He waved his hand to acknowledge me, then spoke:

'Word with you, boss?'

Before Goldy could answer, I was on my feet. Goldy didn't get up, but he held out his hand. When I took it, he put his other hand over mine. We had – I am inclined to mock it, dismiss it in jargon – 'significant eye-contact'. But really that's what we had. I saw, thought I saw, that he understood all where Russell was concerned, perhaps forgave most of it. What he saw in me, I can't say. I hope it wasn't anything too bad. If it was, I would never have the chance to change his mind, for it was the last time we were ever to see each other.

'Wait for me,' Russell murmured as I went past him.

I couldn't speak too well. I was still lost in my conversation with Goldy. They hadn't brought tears on the scale of Johnny Blake's, but I was pretty choked up certainly.

'Think I'll go home,' I managed at last.

'No. Stay. Come up to the fair. We'll have a chat.'

He went in to join Goldy. I passed into the lounge to find the remains of brunch had been cleared away. The long tables were being used for card-games. I didn't need to look to know they would be limited to gin rummy and pontoon. Goldy did not permit casual games of poker under his roof, knowing that they provided far too easy a way for the unwary and unskilled to lose a lot of money fast. Every fortnight he hosted an all-night poker game at which the stakes were high and the action scary. It was rumoured the price of a house could be in the pot of a single hand. Attendance on these nights was strictly by invitation only. None of Goldy's young men was allowed in. I believed Russell had been pressed to attend several times, but had always declined.

I watched a game of rummy for a while. Thought about going home, but the prospect of my empty, silent flat appealed not at all. Instead I left the lounges and went upstairs to the TV room. There were a couple of researchers in there watching a football match, and a researcher's wife who was necking with French Henri. I don't believe her husband was one of the football fans, but am not a hundred per cent certain. Having nothing else to do, I sat down to watch the game and after a while Henri too got involved in what he could see of it past his current partner's hair, and pushed her away to get a better look. Pouting, she left the room.

I can't remember who was in the game – Wolves maybe? Arsenal? After the first five minutes, I didn't see much of it, spending the time rather in thinking over what I had said to Goldy and what it would mean for me in the future. At some time I must have nodded off, for the next thing I remember is that the TV screen was blank and people were milling about, getting ready to go out.

This seemed my cue to start for home. I went downstairs to the cloakroom and lifted my donkey-jacket down from the hook. Putting it on, I turned to find Russell standing behind me.

'Ready?' he said.

'What for?'

'Aren't you coming up to the fair?'

I shook my head.

'Come on. It'll be a laugh.'

I muttered something about buses, trains, it was getting late.

'Bollocks. It's still daylight. And I'll send you home in a taxi, how's that?' We stood facing each other in silence.

Some sort of struggle was going on between us. I had never known him to put this sort of social pressure on anyone, certainly not on me. People could do what they liked, and go where they liked and it was all fine with him, was Russell's usual attitude. Except, it occurred to me suddenly – for I was remembering his persistent wooing of his constituency – when he really wanted something. 'Walk up to the heath with me, Vincent,' he said at last, as close to imploring me as I would ever hear from him. 'Then you can go home.'

III

Most people were going up to the fair on foot – it was only a few hundred yards away, though all uphill certainly. But several of the gangsters found themselves unable to go even that far without the aid of their motors. They left 'Heath's Edge' in a spray of rubber and asphalt, each accompanied by his attendant researcher (who I was coming more and more to see as imps of mischief, sitting on their unwary victims' shoulders). Also Val left in one of these cars. Goldy stayed behind, pleading tiredness, the need to take a nap. (And I don't remember the future Professor Sir Ivor Trasker making the trip either. He had lost at least £5 that day at rummy and, a notoriously sore loser, he must have gone home in a huff when the game folded, a fact which, ever since, he seems to have been at pains to hide. The climax, the denouement to his whole study, and he manages to miss it! Not perhaps a man for the big occasion.)

As we walked, all the sights and scents of the end of a

perfect spring day were spread around us. The trees, which in the winter months seemed to me always taller and blacker and more gaunt here than in other parts of London, were now softened with new buds and early leaves. Darkness was coming on, but just now the sky was still the lightest of blues, the clouds drifting across it the purest of white. A pair of swifts, who may have arrived only this day from Africa, whizzed above the trees before us as straight as if they were riding on tramlines. Here on earth our party, all clad in the vivid clashing tones of the era, stretched out in a long colourful straggle. There was, I remember thinking, something very familiar, and almost immemorial about the picture we made. Over the years, the centuries, groups like ours must have wandered up these hills towards the heath, and probably with the same sort of festive destination in mind. Yes, I thought we might resemble a little Chaucer's travelling pilgrims in our many-hued motley. Like them we were a pretty noisy, talkative crowd: as usual a fair amount of drink had been taken at brunch. A concoction of Guinness and champagne called Black Velvets was a speciality of Goldy's castle on these occasions, and most people here had had a few.

Russell and I walked by ourselves towards the back of the group. I was free to entertain all these fancies, Chaucer and so on, because for some time we walked in absolute silence. Having made, by his standards, such a fuss about having me accompany him, he seemed oddly uninterested in talking to me. In the end I was the one who broke the silence. I tried to make my approach to the subject that I supposed was on both our minds as subtle as I could.

'So where's Anthea today?'

'Bromley. Took the kids to see her mum. Won't be back till late.'

'So you're safe for this evening?'

'I'm what?'

'I'm not going to tell her anything,' I said. He turned to look at me. 'If that's what you're worried about . . . You *should* be worried.' I think I actually tossed my head at this moment in an unlikely gesture of scorn. Then: 'You're an idiot, Russell. How could you risk losing someone like Anthea – for somebody like Val?'

I think he was too surprised by this turn of events – *me* lecturing him about *his* conduct – to have anything immediately to say. I pressed home my rare advantage.

'I'm not going to tell her. But she's going to find out, she's bound to.' Now I was beginning to find his lack of response unsettling. Also the persistence of his surprised expression. 'Well, isn't this what you wanted to talk to me about?'

'What I wanted to talk to you about,' he said heavily, 'is Mum and Dad's anniversary. We ought to do something special. I'd like to know if you had any ideas.'

Forty years married. Ruby anniversary. It called for something special, that's for sure. Only it hadn't been on my mind just then.

'Bruce Forsyth's got a show on at the Palladium,' Russell went on. 'Mum likes him, doesn't she? Not sure about Dad. Is he the one Dad called a disgrace to every normal Englishman?'

'I think that was Kenneth Williams.'

'So the Palladium would be OK? And dinner in town afterwards?'

'Maybe before. Dad can hardly keep his eyes open after ten o'clock nowadays.'

'Right. Dinner before. I'll book it.'

'I'll pay my share, of—'

'Oh, forget it.'

We walked on a few more paces, now in grim silence. Glancing at him, I had no doubt that he was coldly furious with me. I waited to hear him, a certain sinking feeling making its presence known in my stomach. I could hear the rumbling down there even above the chatter and laughter from our companions up ahead.

'What the fuck do you think you're doing, slagging me off about my marriage?'

I don't know why but I did not crumple up immediately under his attack. Perhaps it was that my glimpse of Russell hiding in a closet, fondling his girlfriend, had given me a charge of moral superiority.

'You've slagged me off about my marriage.'

'When did I?'

I reminded him of just when he had, with particular reference to the advice he had given me once about what I should have done to stop my wife removing our baby from the country.

'I didn't mean you should have done anything like that. Not exactly,' Russell said, implicitly conceding that I had a point, he had at least once spoken out against my marriage.

'That's good, 'cause it would have landed me in jail in no time.'

'I just meant you should have fought for the kid a bit, Vincent. Not just laid back and let it happen. You could have done something. You got rights. There are courts.'

'Matty had already gone. Taken the baby with her. All I had was a letter on the kitchen table when I came home from work. They were already on a plane, halfway to the States.'

'There are courts in the States too.'

'Where would I get the money for that?'

'From me? You could have come to me, Vincent. You didn't even think of it, did you?'

I felt such a weight of misery to hear this. I felt another few moments of this and there'd be nothing left of me at all. Not only unfortunate, but culpable, cowardly. I had let the child go without even a struggle. It was true, there was no hiding from it. My spirit struggled to survive. My only defence, I was sure, was in attack.

'That's history. That's over.' I was gasping for air. Russell was even looking a little concerned. 'What about you?'

'What about me?'

'What about you throwing away your life with a really nice woman?' I was feeling a little better now. 'What about Anthea?'

'Didn't know she had such a fan here,' Russell commented.

'Don't be smart. I'm thinking of you.' Actually I was thinking . . . I couldn't put a name to quite what I was thinking, but all at once I lost my appetite for giving Russell good advice. If he wanted to destroy his marriage to a fine and beautiful woman like Anthea, and force her back into the ranks of unattached, available women, well then . . .

Well, then.

Russell at last though seemed touched by my concern. As

we walked the last few yards before the heath came in view, he put his hand on my arm.

'You're not to worry, Vincent,' he said. 'I've got some things to sort out. It hasn't been so easy to let Val go – actually it's been like hell.' And I think if my mind hadn't been somewhat on other things, on certain, almost unthinkable opportunities that might be opening up for me, I would have seen in my brother's face that he wasn't just talking glibly then. It had been like hell for him. As events were to show, this feeling for Val was serious – what had he called her once, his 'soul-mate'? – and it was going to be the devil to extricate himself. 'My fault, I know,' he went on then, 'but I'm gonna do my best to see nobody gets hurt. Especially the boys.'

'But it might mean you'll split with Anthea?'

'It might. I hope not . . . I'm not sure.'

Russell uncertain. Russell in a muddle, not knowing where to turn. Things that would have been inconceivable a few days, even a few hours before. I felt the world turning under me as we rose to the crest of the hill. The great grassy plateau spread out before us. In the last few minutes, without our noticing, night had arrived in the eastern sky. Above us it was still bright, but in the far distance, from the other side of the heath, darkness was spreading. About a quarter of a mile in that direction the lights of the fair shone red and yellow and orange against the black. We could hear the music rolling towards us from the loud-speakers. I think it was a Kinks number.

'I always liked that song,' said Russell. And I said, 'I suppose, if you're going to split up with her, it was a shrewd idea to wait till after the adoption meeting.'

That effectively spoiled the atmosphere of brotherly good feeling that had grown between us over the past few minutes. We walked in silence towards the fair. When we arrived at its outskirts he turned off without a word towards the dodgem cars and – I guessed – wherever he'd arranged to meet Val. I went to hang out near the coconut shy. I always liked watching that.

IV

Time passed. I wandered on my own in the crowd among the rides and side-shows. I went on the Ghost Train, threw darts at some playing cards, had a go on the Whip and the Big Wheel. I bought some candy floss. From time to time as I strolled I caught glimpses of other of Goldy's recent guests. Johnny Blake, his spirits completely restored, was fishing for goldfish. I did not like to think of the fate of any creature in Johnny's hands – swallowing it would be the least terrible option – and hurried on. French Henri was going up the steps into the Ghost Train in the company of a researcher's wife – not the same wife he had been snogging in the TV room. I saw Val a couple of times. Once on her own as far as I could see, the second time over near Madame Melissa's fortune-telling booth with my brother. They were standing facing each other, talking, very intently it looked like. I hurried on from this spectacle too.

Everywhere I went I noticed the usual commingling of gangsters and researchers and, as ever, it appeared that the researchers were behaving more recklessly and unlawfully than their subjects. I happened on a squabble at the hoopla, for instance. The stall-owner was objecting loudly to something that a spotty-faced college-boy, who I only ever knew as 'Buckley', had done. I think he had leaned over the barrier and forced the hoop down over a tin of cigarettes instead of trying to throw it on in the customary fashion. Buckley's argument, as far as I could hear it, was that the hoops would never go over the prizes that way, they weren't designed to. Not the point at all, the stall-owner was arguing, that just wasn't the way the game was played and, keeping myself safely on the far edges of the argument, I had to silently agree with him. However, Buckley's gangster – it was Mikey Fanshaw – stuck up for his researcher as he was bound to. I thought he didn't show much enthusiasm though, which was understandable for the stall-owner was a menacing-looking fellow, one of those barrel-shaped articles with the sleeves rolled high up to display the massive arms and the lurid tattoos. Bald-headed, except for a greasy pony tail. Looked like an old-time naval coxswain of the brutal tendency: a century and a half ago he would have been combing these parts on behalf of a press-gang.

'You said what?' said Mikey, backing away from this hulk. 'Just say that again, you tosser.'

Whatever it was, the stall-owner said it again. Mikey's college-boy nemesis was dancing around, squealing out such stuff as 'That's telling him!' and 'Go on, Mikey – hit him!' It seemed Mikey had nothing left to do but offer himself up for a sacrifice. Luckily for him, the arrival just then of not only French Henri, but Nick Gobelins and another thug whose name I had never caught changed the situation entirely. I got away before too much of the stall-owner's blood was shed; the last I saw, he was on his knees and retching from a couple of blows to the stomach, one each from Mikey and Nick. 'Hit him again!' Buckley was shrieking.

After this it was a restful interlude to stand by the dodgems and watch the people bashing into each other. This, I decided, was the true soul of the fair. The little cars and their noisy occupants, happily playing at violence. Nimbly from car to car leaped the young men who worked the ride, taking money, making change. They balanced on the rear of the cars, swaying from side to side, appearing invulnerable – though nobody certainly would ever risk deliberately trying to dislodge them by smashing into another car when they were aboard it.

At least, I thought, with a tremor of anxiety, nobody currently here would risk it. There were some people I knew out there in the shadows beyond the dodgem track's lights who would be eager to try just such a foolish stunt. But they hadn't found their way here yet and I planned to be gone before they did. Briefly I wondered how the hoopla man was getting on. Then forgot about him. What can't be cured, must be endured – as my late wife Bubbles used often to say – and fortunately this time, not by me.

V

'Fancy a go?' said a familiar voice behind me as the ride ended, the electricity died on the cars.

I turned to find my brother – alone – grinning at me. He nodded towards a couple of nearby cars which were just being vacated by their occupants. In the front car had been two girls. They were now being surrounded by the three boys who'd been in the other car, and had been literally hot on their tails all through the ride. The girls were giggling and protesting now, the boys were laughing and boasting. It was all normal, innocent fun.

'OK,' I said.

We each took a car. A short wait until every other car had been filled, and then the electricity came back on. The poles above our heads crackled. We began to move, slowly at first then picking up speed.

Bang! I looked behind me. Russell had caught me. I waved my hand in acknowledgement. Spun away from him. Raced the length of the track, taking a couple of nudges from other cars on my way, and hitting one myself. A father and daughter combo. I gave them quite a shock. Looking back, I saw that Russell was busy handing over money to the young tough who had landed on his bumper. Shoulder-length black hair with a crimson bandanna tied around it, he balanced expertly behind Russell, picking coins out of his grungy jeans. I saw my brother point to me, and understood he was paying for my ride too. That wouldn't win him any mercy points, I grinned to myself. I loitered up my end of the track for a bit, hiding myself somewhat behind other cars. A couple of challenges were offered to me, but I spun out of their way. Biding my time. Then I saw that the young man had jumped off Russell's car. It was my chance. He didn't see me until too late. I hit him full-on. He was thrown back in his seat. The young man, making change now on another, nearby car, shouted a warning at me. But I didn't care. It was glorious. Russell was a good few seconds sorting himself out. Then he looked over at me, hovering nearby, ready to renew the attack. He grinned at me ruefully, then in a move I hadn't anticipated, spun on his wheels, got to one side of another car that was passing, and shifted it into my path, completely blocking me. He continued his forward movement and I was trying to disentangle myself from the car he had pushed into me. I was desperately aware that he was completing a half-circle that would expose me to a direct attack from the rear. I would be helpless. Oh God, it was going to hurt!

At that moment, we heard the shots. Three of them – one-two-three. Unmistakably gun-shots. Even someone like myself who had never heard the like before – and surely most people there were in the same situation – knew what they were. It hardly needed the screams of horror that followed them to punch the message home. The guy in charge of the ride switched it off. People in the cars got out, clustered on the edge of the track looking out across the crowd towards where the noises had come from. There was a roaring sound from over there now. One of the young men who had been taking money passed near me.

'That's where the shooting-gallery is,' he was saying. 'That's all it is.'

But nobody seemed to believe him. I looked around to see what Russell made of it. He wasn't there. His dodgem car sat motionless like the rest, and empty. Looking up I just caught a glimpse of my brother on the ground, disappearing fast into the crowd, heading towards where the sound of gunfire had come from.

Fifteen

I

Her coffin had been carried into the chapel by the undertaker's men. It rested on a trestle now, a short distance from where Vincent was sitting in the front row of benches. He had not thought to enquire exactly how in this establishment it was customary to deliver the body to its destruction. At the only other cremation service he'd ever attended – an aunt's, thirty years ago – the coffin, which appeared to be balanced on circular brass cylinders, had been made by the press of a button to roll backward through a pair of swing doors beyond which he was sure he had seen sudden gushes of flame flare out to greet the remains. A hot breath of air had passed across the faces of the mourners. Then the swing doors had closed again, cutting them off from all further contact with the infernal region.

The process had seemed to Vincent then such a strange and macabre combination of the primitive and the mechanical, and now – as he drifted in and out of a reverie in which memories of Bubbles had mingled not uncomfortably with mild worries about whether or not Rob would be staying for lunch, and if there was enough food in the house if he was – he checked each time he looked up to see if he could detect any ominous signs yet, any buttons, rollers, swing doors. But there were none. None that he could see, and he concluded at last that whatever was going to happen would not happen here. She would be taken somewhere else, somewhere discreet, hidden from the public gaze, and the deed done there. Which was how she would have wanted it, and certainly how he did.

Something else he had forgotten to check, he remembered, was exactly what form this ceremony was going to take given that his instructions to the undertaker had been that there should be no ceremony at all. For a moment here he had felt a stab of panic, imagining that the result of such a refusal to give directions must be a void, something without form, chaos at worst. But after a few moments of preliminary milling around, it was apparent that the occasion would be spared the worst results of his dereliction. Finding no order, the mourners imposed it on themselves. They filed in through the chapel doors, and took their places along the benches without scuffling for precedence. Two of their number elected themselves as ushers and began greeting each new arrival in an appropriately sober and authoritative fashion, and directing them to the remaining empty places.

Soon there were not many of those, and in a while there were none at all, except in the front row where Vincent and Rob were respectfully left to sit and grieve alone. Elsewhere it was cheek to jowl, buttock to buttock. Still more people were trying to come in. They were left to stand around at the back. SRO for Bubbles. From time to time Vincent tried to catch a glimpse of individuals in the ranks behind him. It was hard. Each glance caught just a blur of faces. He *thought* there was possibly a bunch of people from the old constituency days, both Labour and SDP, sitting about half-a-dozen rows back. Couldn't be sure of that though. And certainly he couldn't find in any of his brief glimpses the only face he was truly searching for, the one he also dreaded to see. He couldn't find Russell anywhere.

A woman he had never seen before appeared in front of him suddenly. Early middle-age, wearing a trim, dark-grey suit, rather good-looking. In fact just the type of woman he had fantasised having sex with quite often during Bubbles' last months when that sort of thing was pretty much out of the question between them. It was curious, he had never daydreamed in this time about the girls or young women that the magazines and advertisements told him should form the substance of his fantasies, but always about such a one as this: between thirty-eight and forty-five, alluring without being aggressive, inviting without being demanding, conventionally even strictly dressed but in such a way that nobody – not Vincent anyway – could ignore the fine full female body that was beneath the cloth. Remembering now some of the details of those imaginary encounters gave him the beginnings of quite a little hard-on. He crossed his legs protectively.

This present incarnation of his libidinous reveries, clearly having no idea of the state he was in, gave him an encouraging smile and then, bowing her head and clasping her hands together in a position which was not quite that of prayer, began to speak in a quiet and friendly voice.

'This is a sad occasion, of course, for all of us – so many of us! – who knew and loved the person who has departed from our midst. Yet it is also in a way a comforting time, even a joyous one, reasserting as it does our connection to all that is human, the living and the dead, one unbroken thread of humanity, stretching across the ages that go back to our very beginnings and stretching forth through all the ages that lie ahead. Here, in this brief moment of time, we catch the thread in our hands, we hold it, we feel its strength and majesty, and then, as we must, we let it go.'

Vincent, while wanting very much to respond appropriately to this call to reflect upon the profound and serious mysteries of life, was unable to stop himself fretting over whether or not he would be charged for it. He was certain he hadn't ordered it. In fact, he remembered specifically declining the services of any speaker – religious, humanist, anybody – during his interview with the undertaker. And he had sat in enough restaurants during the old parliamentary days totting up the bill after the meal and finding the odd unordered starter, or the liqueurs that had been requested but had never actually appeared, to fall for that one. Bubbles could never be bothered, and in fact had often made fun of him sitting there, his glasses low on his nose, scanning the bill, doing sums in his head, the waiter frowning belligerently behind him. 'What does it matter,' she'd say. 'It was a good meal.' Yet he reckoned he'd found a miscalculation – to put it kindly – on at least one bill in five. Say, they ate out in those days at most two nights a week (more when the House was sitting), then the average savings per year, given what eating out cost back then . . . he worked on the sum now, frowning over the unaccustomed mental effort.

He looked up at some point to find the woman regarding him steadily and with great compassion. With some shame he realised that she was interpreting his visible struggles over the arithmetic he was doing as evidence of a turbulent personal distress. He composed his features, tried to look less like a man at the complete end of his tether. Addressing him directly, she said:

'There is a poem that I love. It was written by a man on the last day of his life and on the surface is full of despair. And yet I've often found that the verses can be a resource in times of great sorrow, for beneath the agitated surface they speak to us so clearly of the calmness and resignation that we all must discover in ourselves if we are to find the way through such sorrowful times as these. And if we are truly to know and accept that the distant harbour our dear friend has now reached waits for us too:

> '*I sought my death* (the woman said), *and found it in my*
> *womb*
> *I looked for life and saw it was a shade;*
> *I trod the earth and knew it was my tomb,*
> *And now I die, and now I was but made.*
> *My glass is full, and now my glass is run,*
> *And now I live, and now my life is done.*'

Before she'd finished, Vincent's head was drooped in the nearest thing he could approach to prayer. He felt such grief, it was as if he had never felt it really before. Not when Bubbles had first told him she was ill, not when it was clear she was dying, nor when she did die. He wanted so much now to cry. He had everything ready in him to cry, yet the tears would not come. He prayed instead:

'Bubbles, I am so glad that you are dead. The last month or so was bloody miserable for you. Though I think you felt nothing much towards the very end, not even pain. Certainly your death came so easily that I did not notice exactly when it happened. I had turned away to look at something on the television – it was a darts match, John Lowe had to make 76 to win it, needed double eighteen to finish it off. I watched him do it, nice throw John, and when I looked back you had left me. In the time it took for a dart to leave a hand and hit the board.

'And I was glad for you. It had gone on too long. Enough. For God's sake, enough.

'But oh Bubbles *what am I going to do now?*'

That was a shriek of real pain at the end. Suddenly horrified, he feared that the grief he felt, the tears he couldn't cry, his actual prayers were all for him, not for his wife at all. What selfishness. What sad, sick behaviour – he looked up as if hoping that the woman had another verse handy to get him over this particular difficult bit. She wasn't there, she had disappeared. Only the coffin in front of him, on its trestle.

Oh, he felt so bad. As if streams of pain were flowing from his eyes, his ears, from everywhere. He began rocking in his seat, forward and back. He felt pressure on his arm then. Then nothing. Then felt it again. He looked sideways. Rob was nudging him.

'What?'

'Go up and say a word, Dad.'

Vincent regarded the space where he had seen the woman. (Had she ever really been there? Doubtful, he decided. Very doubtful. He knew that poem though. They'd had to learn it at school: 'My prime of youth is but a frost of cares/My feast of joy is but a dish of pain . . .' Oh, yes, indeed. 'The day is past and yet I saw no sun/And now I live, and now my life is done . . .' Etcetera. Would you credit making twelve-year-olds memorise *that*? His generation had been surely raised by maniacs.)

'Why me?'

'Dad – it's got to be you first.'

Slowly, appalled at what he was doing, Vincent struggled to his feet. Rob got up with him and made sure he was steady. Then sat down again. Vincent stepped forward a couple of paces, then turned. All these pairs of eyes staring at him. Hundreds of pairs, it felt like. Probably was.

'Thank you all for coming here,' he began haltingly. At that moment he caught sight of Baz Jacobson sitting in the third row. Bald now, with a rabbinical black beard, but undeniably Baz. Vincent was so shocked to see him, that he forgot entirely what he was doing. Rob leaned forward after about half a minute of total silence.

'Dad?' he murmured.

'Yes,' said Vincent. He dragged his gaze away from Baz. Let it travel over the rest of the audience. So many once-familiar faces he saw now. Where the hell had all these people been in the last years of her life? If they'd had a couple of visitors in a month it was a phenomenon. 'Some of you,' he said, his gaze still wandering about the room, amazed, 'will know that towards the end of her life my wife – Bubbles – became addicted –'

He stopped to clear his throat. Then noticed that the

room had got very quiet, people were straining to hear what he had to say next.

'– became addicted,' he went on quickly, 'to the telling of jokes. The filthier the better actually. There was one that was her special favourite. It may be new to some of you here present.' He closed his eyes for a moment, wanting to get it straight in his mind, to do Bubbles justice. 'It seems there was this holiday camp – on the coast somewhere, Kent, I think it was, maybe Sussex – and one night, for the entertainment of the guests, the staff decided to hold a big prick contest . . . Or was it a tight minge contest? . . . Anyway, be that as it may –'

Rob got to him before he could say much more. Which was fortunate because he felt he was going to collapse at any moment. He was swaying – Rob caught him.

'Come on, Dad,' he said. 'You've done enough.'

Together they went up the narrow aisle between the silent, seated ranks of mourners and then pushed through the crowd at the back of the room. Vincent kept his head down almost all the way, not wanting to confront the torrent of contempt and dislike that he guessed must be flowing towards him from all those pairs of eyes. He only looked up once at the very back of the room as they were leaving it, but too briefly to confirm that his guess had been correct.

II

Rob broke the bad news as they drove out of the crematorium and joined the main road.

'A reception?' breathed Vincent, horrified.

'Well, we couldn't get all those people along to the funeral and not give them something to eat and drink afterwards.'

'I didn't want them at the funeral in the first —'

'It's all right, Dad. You don't have to do a thing. It's all taken care of, the caterers — everything.'

'No! I won't allow it.'

'Now, Dad—'

'You had no right.'

'She's my—'

'I don't care that she's your mother. I know what she would have wanted. And what she *wouldn't* have wanted is for all those bastards to see where we were living at the end. It was all right for us, but — well, you know what it's like. Bloody Rodney's music, and the smell on the stairs, and how poky it is. She was very proud, Rob, she would have hated people to have seen—'

'But, Dad—'

'Is that turd Jacobson planning to show up?'

'Sir Baz? I believe so.'

'Never. I forbid it.'

'Oh, come on, Dad. Baz has been very helpful. It was him who found that woman to give the address. And he paid for her.'

'You mean that woman existed?'

'What?'

'. . . No, Rob, I won't allow it. He threatened Bubbles' life once. He said she should get cancer. I will not have him in our home. No.'

'But that's the point, Dad. Like I said it's all taken care of.

Lord Worthington offered his penthouse apartment for the reception. I believe it's huge. Beside the river. Next building to Jeffrey Archer's. I bet Mum would have been so pleased to have her reception there.'

'Who the hell is Lord Worthington?'

'Come on, Dad, you were telling me about him. He danced with Mum at the SDP conference?'

'*Malcolm* Worthington? My God! That creep? He was such a pain in the neck. SDP MP. Came in on a by-election. Totally unexpected. He was furious. He'd only stood because he was sure he would lose. All he wanted was to go back to his job, running some sort of purchasing agency up in Darlington for the old British Rail. Very fed-up he had to hang around Westminster for a couple of years instead. The place frightened him to bits. Bubbles had to take him under her wing. Of course she despised him really. Whining, over-grown baby . . . *And* he put his hand on her behind, I saw him do it. Now he's Lord Worthington? Who made him a peer?'

'I think the present lot. He said they'd given him a job.'

'Ah, he went over to the enemy finally, did he?'

'He said on the phone he has nothing but happy memories of you and Mum and the old times in the House. "Famous days," he kept saying. "They were famous days".'

'Famous bollocks.' Vincent brooded for a bit. 'Your mother should have got out of the Party when the going was good. Made friends with some other mob. Jack Rolls is right. We should have done anything, cheated, sold out, kissed any available arse, just to stay in the sun. She'd have been sitting in the House of Lords too all these years.

Baroness Bubbles. It would have been a kind of life, or after-life. Better than what she had . . . It's my fault. I encouraged her to stay true. That was our pride. We never turned traitor. Idiots.'

'Did you see the flowers at the crematorium from Dr Owen?'

'I didn't.'

'They were very nice.'

'That was her reward. Bunch of flowers. No,' said Vincent after a moment's reflection, 'it was good of him to remember. Good of Lord Owen. He would have been there today of course, but he's abroad just now. Malaysia, I think. A fact-finding mission. Or Cambodia, one or the other. I had a good phone call from there the morning after she died. Somebody back here must have been detailed to keep him up-to-date on the situation. It was typically thoughtful of him . . . But even so,' Vincent went on, as a new rush of resentment overtook him, 'it's not right. Bloody Gang of Four. All right, so things didn't work out just as they wanted, but they've all ended up doing pretty well, thank-you. And a few others have, like Worthington. But what about the rest of us? Suckers like Bubbles and me. What happened to us after the crash?'

'You were happy together,' Rob said. 'You and Mum. I always thought that.'

Vincent said at last, 'Why don't you drop me off at a bus stop, Rob? You should go back to the crematorium. One of her sons should be there to see everyone out.'

'It's OK, Dad. Tim can do it for both of us.'

'. . . *Tim* was there? Tim came to her funeral?'

'That's right. Didn't you see him? Sitting next to Russell?'

'No. I didn't. Did he come to gloat?'

Rob refused to dignify that with an answer. Vincent studied the passing scenery. They were up near the river by now, well out of his home territory.

'Take me home, Rob.'

'What? But I explained—'

'Just take me home. Have your reception. Say hello to everyone from me, but I want to go home now. I've had enough.'

'But—'

'Do you really think I'm in a fit state to attend a reception? I just tried to tell a dirty joke at your mother's funeral.'

'Yes. Any idea why you did that?'

He had none. No idea. Nothing to say.

'Anyway – it wasn't so bad.'

'If it wasn't so bad, why did you stop me and get me out of there?'

'It was the way you were telling it. I thought you looked—'

'At the end of my tether?'

'Sort of. But I don't think anybody really minded. In fact one guy was even clapping. Did you see him on the way out? Poncey-looking bloke in a leather bomber jacket and a white silk scarf.'

'That would be Terence Farquarson. He used to be Bubbles' agent. He's mine now, I suppose. Clapping, was he? I guess he felt he had to do that. Support the client, you know. However bad the disaster. Please take me home, Rob.'

'People'll be so disappointed.'

'That's all right. I'm disappointed, why shouldn't they be?'

'And Russell is really looking forward to seeing you again. He's set his heart on it.'

'Ah, has he? Well, too bad. I can't face him, Rob. We haven't seen each other for a quarter of a century. What's the point now?' He thought it over, then: 'And Tim? Is he going to be there too? Bubbles would have forgiven him for abandoning her, but I can't. I won't. I certainly don't want to talk to him.'

'That's OK. Tim doesn't want to talk to you either.'

'Oh, he doesn't? Well, sod him. D'you know I used to take that kid along to watch bloody Charlton Athletic every other Saturday afternoon, winter after winter after bloody winter. And I hate football . . . Rob – *take me home.*'

III

Inside the flat, Rob went straight to the room he'd slept in. Vincent hovered near the door. It wasn't closed shut, there was an inch or two of space between it and the jamb. He could see his son moving around in the room, but not exactly what he was doing. It was not like Rob to hide himself away like this, for a sulk. Not like the grown-up Rob, he corrected himself then; the teenage one had used to sulk for England.

'Rob,' he called through the gap, 'there's no need for you to miss the reception too. Just go. I'll be OK.'

'I'm planning to go,' he heard then.

'Ah, OK . . . well, I may go to bed early. I'll leave the door off the latch, shall I?'

No reply. This was ridiculous. Vincent pushed open the door. Rob had his overnight case on the bed, he was just finishing zipping it up. He looked round at Vincent in the doorway.

'Rob, this isn't necessary. Don't be angry with me.'

'I'm not angry.'

'I know you wanted this to be some sort of great reconciliation. But it's not on. Don't you see that?' Vincent sighed. 'Oh, maybe I should do it for you. Go to this bloody reception. If I was a better father . . . But I just can't do it.'

'Fair enough.'

'Fair enough?' He hesitated. 'Will you come back here then? I'll stay up for you, shall I? I've got some whisky somewhere. We'll get sloshed, have a good talk?'

'Can't do it, Vincent. I've got to be back in Belfast tonight. Dad and Tim are driving me straight to the airport after the reception.'

It was nothing. A plan. A commonsensical set of arrangements. And he'd called Vincent 'Vincent' and Russell 'Dad'. But it was as if in that moment he had pronounced his final allegiance. Now that Bubbles was dead, he didn't have to pretend any more. He could show himself in his true livery. And so Vincent had no sons at all now. One of them he had abandoned all hopes for long ago and good riddance, but, oh, this one would hurt.

Rob turned back to the bed to straighten the covers. Vincent thought to tell him it didn't matter, he'd do it. But he couldn't be bothered now. Also he was suddenly preoccupied by the clearest of memories: of Rob's friend, Sergeant Hurry, sitting on this bed. Not in this room, that was in another house, but this same bed. He could remember him on it, turning and laughing at something Bubbles had just said to him. They, Bubbles and Vincent, were standing in the doorway. Watching Hurry on the bed. Now dead.

(Though not, after all, killed by the IRA as he and Bubbles had first surmised when they heard the news. Tobogganing accident in the Austrian Alps.)

Dead. Bed. Rob's lover, perhaps . . .

Rob picked up his overcoat. He turned to get hold of his case.

'Let me carry that downstairs.'

'It's OK—'

'I'll carry it,' Vincent insisted.

At the car, he held his hand out. 'Goodbye then,' he said. 'And thank you for being here.' Rob didn't move, only stared at him from out of the window. 'Won't you shake hands with me, Rob?'

At last, Rob did. 'It's a pity,' he said, letting go. 'I organised this whole bloody reception for you.'

'No, you didn't, but it was a nice idea. Enjoy yourself. Give Baz a kick in the balls from me . . . Oh, Rob,' he cried out then, 'I feel I'm never going to see you again, never going to hear from you—'

'Don't be daft, Dad,' Rob said crisply. 'It's your birthday next week. I'll give you a call as usual.'

Vincent stepped away, watched the car go. Taking his son. The lucky boy with two dads. He watched until it disappeared around the bend in the road, then turned back towards his house.

Sixteen

I

Soon after I had seen Russell running from the dodgem ride towards the gun-shots, I proved myself to be, just like Ivor Trasker, not at all a man for the big occasion by turning in the opposite direction when I got down to ground-level and heading towards the blackness beyond the fair. I was aiming for a cluster of lamps in about the centre of the heath. Beyond that I would be able to see the church clearly, and beyond that would be the safety of the village itself. I couldn't exactly say why I was scuttling away so fast. Nobody was after me, nobody certainly had taken shots at *me*. It was just instinct, and plain old-fashioned funk. To the derisive, I would say only that I'm prepared to let my behaviour be judged by the results, and unlike my bold big brother I have not spent a large fraction of my life in a maximum-security prison.

This I heard and saw from my dark and distant and moving vantage-point. Nothing at all for a while. The fairground music – currently a Slade number, I remember – sounded faint and wavering from this distance. At one point it was abruptly cut off. I heard a noise then, like a growl, rolling across the heath. A few moments of silence. Then shouts. I couldn't see too well, but there appeared to be running figures about a hundred yards from where I was,

211

all heading towards the south-west corner of the heath. The figures at first ran in ones and twos. Then a small mob of people went racing past. I had slowed in my flight to watch. There was a gap after the little crowd had gone by. Then a great surge of people, all seemingly shouting at the tops of their voices. I thought I heard police whistles coming from their midst too. Then decided it was a trick of the acoustics up here on this bare plateau, and that the whistles were really coming from back in the fairground.

I wasn't sure what to do. The people had disappeared from my view, yet I could still hear them. I was tempted to go after them, find out what the fuss was all about. But on the other hand . . . Looking around just then, I saw in the glow of the nearby lamps a fox looking at me from beside a rubbish bin. The two of us regarded each other for several seconds. We were both absolutely still. Its lemon eyes gleamed in the lamplight. I caught my breath, transfixed by what must always be the stirring sight of a wild animal near the heart of London. I don't think I even heard the roaring of the crowd any more. Until – the fox seemed to glance over its shoulder at the source. And then turned and, without fuss or apparent fear, trotted out of the pool of light, away from the sound of people. It struck me that this beast knew a thing or two about survival, and what it deemed suitable behaviour in the current situation would probably suit me very well too. I gave it time enough to get well ahead of me, then followed in its wake. In a few minutes I was at Blackheath railway station. I took a train from there to Charing Cross and onward then by tube to my flat, and that was the end of my night out.

Almost everything I know therefore about the notorious events of that evening has had to be pieced together from the testimony of witnesses better placed than myself, or from accounts in the newspapers (the least reliable source), or from the evidence that was produced at the trial (running the newspapers neck-and-neck sometimes for unreliability, and often outright mendacity, at least when it concerned the police evidence). A lot of it came from muttered conversations with those of Goldy's young men who would risk talking to me. From their employer I never heard directly. He wouldn't speak to me on the phone, wouldn't answer my letters, wouldn't come to the door on the couple of occasions I called at his castle. I got messages through other people from him certainly. They ranged from the early: 'Tell Vincent, when the fuss has died down we'll get it sorted out, not to worry' to the late 'It's a bloody shame; but what the hell can *I* do?'

'Goldy's trying to distance himself,' Nick Gobelins explained to me one evening when I was standing in the porch of his master's house. He had just prevented me intruding on it any further, mainly by putting his body between me and the half-opened door.

'Oh, really? Is that what he's doing?' Bitterness and sarcasm had early entered into my view of Goldy in these post-incident times.

Nick frowned at my attitude. 'Don't be like that, Vincent,' he said.

I stood there, boiling impotently. Nick looked down at me with an amused and tolerant gaze. There seemed to be, I remembered later, something new about Nick's bearing today, some increase in authority and stature. Even his clothes had changed, were more formal, the style subtler, the colours in them more subdued. If I'd noticed these things at the time I would have guessed the truth: that Nick had just received a promotion, and that Russell's place in the gang, however inadequately, had already been filled.

But on the spot I was far too incensed to bother about this.

'Why isn't Goldy doing anything? He could be helping Russell. He knows people; he could be talking to them.'

'Russell send you to say this?'

I shook my head. Nick nodded comfortably.

'Course he didn't. He knows the score. If ever he thought he'd need the guvnor to stand by him, he wouldn't of been knocking off the guvnor's girlfriend, would he?'

So this is what I believe happened that night. It started with Val, who was a bit drunk and quite a lot distressed. There had been some kind of an argument with Russell in the time just before I encountered him at the dodgems. My brother made the decision that they should separate for an hour or so, until calm was restored. Johnny Blake, who was also, as I knew, in a somewhat fragile frame of mind this night, was unluckily deputised by Russell to keep an eye on Val and cheer her up. He did his best. Took her on the Whip. But it made her feel sick. A huge helping of candy floss didn't help much, nor the toffee apple that followed it. Johnny decided that a quieter, less stomach-heaving pastime was required. They went back to the goldfish stall. Rod in hand, Val tried to win one of the prizes, but failed. She was probably too drunk to focus. In the end Johnny had to do it for her.

At some point in their time at this stall, they were joined by Johnny Blake's regular researcher. At this distance, I forget his name. It doesn't appear in any of the written accounts; he was never called to give evidence. But he was to become a major source of information for me in the two hurried, late-night phone conversations we had during the weeks after the incident, both of which ended abruptly when he hung up in the middle of one of his sentences.

Anyway, as they left the goldfish stall, this researcher was given the little fish to carry inside its plastic bag. (There was only one plastic bag in the frame, my informant insisted, one fish – what had happened to the previous specimen Johnny had won he had no idea.) Johnny then asked Val what she wanted to do now. To see Russell, was her answer. He told her she could do that when Russell said it was OK, but not before. Meanwhile – how about the shooting gallery, which their meandering course had now brought them to? It was an unremarkable facility called, as I read afterwards in the papers, 'Lash Arizona's Dry Gulch Shooting Academy'. The usual row of metal ducks moved slowly along the back of the stall. There were four or five airguns chained to the counter. The guy in charge tonight (possibly the actual Lash Arizona, though the name in the papers wasn't anything like that) lounged at the side of the display of prizes. It was the regular deal. When paid, he handed out little slugs for the guns; if you won he gave you a prize depending on how many ducks you'd knocked down. None of the prizes – mostly ceramic stuff, vases and such – was worth winning however many ducks went down, my informant reported. Nevertheless, Val made Johnny buy her a dozen slugs to give herself every chance. She didn't manage to hit any of the ducks but chipped the glaze off several of the prizes. And her ricochets caused the stall-owner to jump around.

Johnny called for another dozen slugs. The stall-owner demurred. He wouldn't do it unless Johnny paid for the prizes that had been damaged, and put down a deposit on any future breakages.

'Do what?' Johnny asked.

The stall-owner shrugged. A thoughtful expression came upon Johnny's face. He seemed, said the researcher, to be weighing up the man before him, reviewing his points of vulnerability. And it might have gone badly then for the stall-owner, worse probably – considering the way Johnny liked to abandon himself to his rages – than it had gone for the hoopla stall man. The researcher felt he ought to intervene.

'I was trying to smooth things over,' he muttered down the phone.

'By suggesting she used a *real gun*?'

Johnny and Val had chuckled at the notion. I hate to think of the next few moments. A drunken, unhappy girl, fast approaching hysteria, an irresponsible college idiot, and a volatile street-boy needing badly to impress anybody within a half-mile radius of himself all rolled downhill towards disaster, unstoppable as a train engine with the brakes off. And I have not even mentioned the almost literally fatal factor in the equation. There was the gun. Whether Johnny Blake's personal weapon, or the solitary item of mischief that, in Russell's opinion, was the total armament of Goldy's troops. If so, Johnny had it now.

Tucked into the waistband of his trousers in the approved manner. How often I wished afterwards that it had gone off accidentally before he could pull it out, and shot off his kneecaps or his balls or any other part of his stupid anatomy.

But he produced it. Showed it to Val.

'Bet I could hit those bloody ducks with that!' she glowed.

'Bet you could, darlin'.' A gallant Irish smile, a wink to the college-boy ('I swear, I couldn't believe it was happening!' was this moron's later gloss on the event), and the gun changes hands. The stall-owner, no fool, ducks for cover. Val takes aim.

Those were the shots that we heard over at the dodgems. The woman's scream that followed was because her child, a boy of three, who she'd been carrying in her arms as she was walking near Lash Arizona's stall, had been hit by a ricochet. It struck him at the top of his arm, not much more than a graze. But there was quite a lot of blood and the child was understandably so shocked by the impact that he fainted clean away. For all the woman knew she was carrying her dead son. She screamed and screamed. She sank to her knees hugging her infant to her. Her other child, a little girl of five or six who had been walking beside her mother, holding on to her free hand, saw all this going on and started yelling herself in emulation. People gathered around, appalled. It appeared as if the whole family had been engulfed in some inexplicable catastrophe.

At this point Val was still holding the gun. Johnny Blake had taken himself out of the scene the moment the woman had started screaming, and in fact was already on the first leg of his journey back to Ulster where he was found at last

– though not, unfortunately for him, by the police – several years later. My informant-researcher was still on the spot, however ('I couldn't move, it was like I was frozen.') Val was staring curiously towards her victims. They were rapidly being shielded from her view by the people clustering around them, trying to help. Nobody had thought to look in her direction yet, but it was only a matter of time before they did. Where the shooting-gallery man was my researcher could not say. Probably still hiding under his table of prizes. Now the crowd opened up for a moment to let two police officers, drawn by the commotion, into the centre of the circle.

At that moment, my brother too appeared out of the crowd. He goes straight to Val, who has begun to cry. He takes the gun from her hand, and puts it in his pocket. Then ('without a glance at me,' said my researcher, sounding aggrieved at the slight), he took her arm and began to walk her steadily away from the scene. She went without a murmur. Nobody seemed to have noticed them, and they might have got away without trouble, except . . .

Somebody *had* noticed them. A woman in the crowd pointed them out to the police. According to these officers' later evidence, she had given on the spot a very believable and circumstantial account of the shooting, in which she placed the gun not in Val's hand, but in Russell's. In fact she seemed to have only the vaguest impression of Val, could not describe her, was not even sure she had been present at the time the shots were fired. In contrast, her description of Russell was detailed and accurate. This woman, in spite of repeated appeals to come forward, was never found afterwards. Nevertheless, her hearsay evidence was allowed to stand at the trial, and by then a half-dozen other 'witnesses', wanting to get in on the act, were ready to swear blind that they too could identify Russell as the one and only shooter.

In any case by pointing out the retreating forms of Russell and Val as they passed through the fairground – so near the blackness by now, so close to safety – the mystery woman had performed her crucial act. People, overhearing her, started to run after the two miscreants in a sort of self-appointed posse. Those were the occasional shapes I first saw running across the heath. Then the police whistles blew to summon help. Behind the officers, a whole mob of people went off in pursuit, though I presume some stayed behind to care for the little family that had been so shocked and damaged. I have a memory that in the course of the trial officers of the St John's Ambulance Brigade were thanked for their exertions that night. My researcher couldn't tell me about this. Seeing safety in numbers, he had joined the second, larger eruption of people out of the fairground and found himself running more or less neck-and-neck with a large police sergeant. In the spirit of competition, my researcher dug deep into himself and being younger and nimbler had soon left the sergeant behind. At that point he had veered to the left and was soon off the Health, and out of the drama, and had no more information to give me concerning the events of that night.

'What happened to the second goldfish?'

'The goldfish?'

'Weren't you carrying it?'

'The goldfish!' he cried somewhat wildly down the phone. '*Christ* knows.'

Russell and Val had run from the fairground across Shooters Hill(!) and down a then little-used lane called Duke Humphrey Road. On either side the heath stretched, dark and empty, and I have often wondered since why they did not turn off into its concealing shadows. I think probably that, two South Londoners, in an emergency they instinctively rejected the wide open spaces and were seeking the familiar sanctuary of streets, houses, council estates, back-alleys. What they were making for initially were probably the lights of the Hare and Billet pub, just north of the Village, and of the streets nearby.

In those days there was a small factory situated a little way behind the pub. I think I may have passed by it on one of those occasions when I'd been visiting Goldy's and had gone out with my brother for a walk on the heath as a break from the eating and partying back at the castle. But I never knew what was made there; or, if I was told, I've forgotten it. In any case the factory buildings have probably gone by now; they were pretty old then, and in a fairly dilapidated and neglected state, and except for a single security light outside the main gate, lay in darkness. There was nothing much else to deter an intruder, and that night Russell and Val intruded. He must have kicked off the padlock that held the gate closed. It was later found broken on the ground outside.

Their pursuers were too close for this refuge to remain undetected. Yet now that the news that one of these criminals (there were still thought to be more than one at this point) was carrying a gun had spread generally, there was no rash pursuit through the gates, into the factory. The early arrivals milled about outside. When the police came they were able to point out where the villains had gone. The numbers of police had swelled to almost a score by now. There were enough to be sent round to find out if there was a rear exit to the factory. At about the time I, down at Blackheath station, was stepping on to my Charing Cross train, the siege began in earnest. Lights were set up. Bull-horns used to call on whoever was inside the factory to surrender. Armed police officers in flak jackets arrived soon after. They were much rarer in those days, and the excite-ment generated by their arrival among the crowd (kept at bay by some of the now fifty or so officers at the scene) became intense.

Everybody agreed it was as good as a film; people could hardly wait for the shooting to start, with the only caveat being that nobody wanted to be in the front-line of specta-tors when it did. There was so much moving, and pushing, and getting behind other people for safety, that hardly anybody noticed that the siege had ended when it did. Something happened though, just beyond the factory gates. Two armed officers went forward, followed at a short distance by a uniformed police inspector. About ten minutes went by, whatever was happening being kept quite out of sight of the crowd. The atmosphere was turning a bit ugly. People were feeling cheated. At that moment, from behind the mob, came the see-sawing moan of a siren. The crowd parted. A police car bumped slowly across the heath and towards the factory gate. It stopped just outside. The driver got out and opened one of the car's rear doors. From behind the gate stepped first a cop holding a rifle, then a man in 'civilian' dress, then another armed officer, who was followed at last by the police inspector. Among the strongest rumours flying around the crowd was that a woman had been somehow involved in this outrage. But that must have been a mistake, for only this man appeared, head down, hiding his guilty features behind his hands. All in the party got into the car, the inspector choosing to ride in front.

At the first sight of the suspect a roar went up from the crowd. Most people in it had only a sketchy idea of what it was he had done, but one assumption gaining ground was that he had killed at least two children, so the mood was understandably full of rage. As the police car tried to get through the people to reach the road, they surrounded it, and beat on the windows and roof. The 'child-killer's' face, startled, peered out at them. The sight drove them to even greater fury. They started to rock the car. It was getting dangerous. Police with batons in their hands had to drive them back from their prey, or somebody would really have got killed that night.

II

In those moments when the 'Monster of Blackheath' (credit next day's *Daily Mirror*) was being driven to safety, I was probably waiting for my tube at the Embankment station. It arrived pretty soon and I was back in my flat within twenty minutes. After watching TV for a bit, I went to bed not long after ten o'clock as I had classes scheduled for early the next morning. Something about the disorderly events of the day that was past – though I had no conception of course to what disastrous ends they'd been heading – had troubled me, and I had some vague ideas of turning over a new leaf in my life. Cleaning up my act, as they say. I would start by making at least a minimal effort to fulfil the responsibilities of my job. An early night would see me up and ready for business first thing in the morning.

At about half an hour after midnight, my phone rang. It was my mother, crying so much I couldn't understand a word she was saying. Then my father came on, and told me about Russell. The police had called at their house. Anthea had also been contacted. She was 'in a state', according to my father. Could I get hold of a taxi and go over there? I didn't make my classes that day, nor for many days after. And by that time it hardly mattered. The decision had been taken to sack me. It was done – regretfully, gracefully – about six weeks before Russell went for trial at the Old Bailey. The younger brother's fate went unnoticed, of course, even by me almost; the older brother's was the talk of the country. Back then, the shooting of a child was an almost unimaginable outrage; it was certainly hot news. Every day outside my parents' shop the placards reported the hearing's progress: 'Stabler Trial Latest' they read. I argued with my father that he didn't have to keep those things out there, but he wouldn't listen to me. He knew about professional responsibilities, even if I didn't. The only time he had ever refused to exhibit a placard had been immediately after the incident on the heath, when the shop had been closed for twenty-four hours. That day the notices had read 'Penge Thug Wounds Three-Year-Old.' Unfairly, I find myself wondering sometimes if it was the word 'thug' as applied to his oldest boy that had most distressed our father, or the word 'Penge'.

As to what happened to Val that night, and subsequently: it was a mystery to me for many years. Nothing was said of her at the trial, nor at any other time. I learned the truth eventually on a day in the mid-Eighties when I happened to meet French Henri on the top of a bus in Brixton High Street. Traffic was slow, and we were able to have a good long talk until he had to get out at Camberwell Green. He seemed to be in pretty good shape. No longer part of the criminal world, he was keen to assure me. Goldy's gang had packed it in even before the leader died. Seeing no more prospects in that direction, Henri had taken a government-sponsored training course in home-appliance repair. He was making a fairly tidy living at it now; as he said, with a £100 calling-out fee every time, he could hardly miss.

Naturally our talk wended round eventually to Russell, and the events of that night on Blackheath. He said that Russell had got Val out of the back of the factory just before the police could block that exit. Then he had gone back to the front to distract the officers out there. Val had headed straight back to Goldy's castle and told all she knew. Goldy had arranged for her to leave the country that same night. She went to Spain; got into the tourist pub business. As far as Henri knew, she was still out there. Goldy had probably given her the money to get started: he never blamed her really for what happened – not like he blamed Russell.

Henri also happened to mention that Johnny Blake was dead. In '79 a bomb blast had ripped apart a car on a country lane outside Portadown. Inside was Johnny's body in several pieces. The official theory was that it was his own bomb and he was on his way to plant it somewhere when it had accidentally detonated. Henri couldn't tell me if anything equally fatal had happened to the third member of the lunatic trio that had gathered around Lash Arizona's that night: my telephone confidant, the researcher. Of course it didn't help in jogging his memory that, as I've said, I couldn't now remember the young man's name.

French Henri explained then, unprompted, that the reason Russell had helped Val out of the factory building, then gone and sacrificed himself to ensure her escape was that he was besotted with her. Same reason for why he had never let his lawyers mention her at the trial. Same reason I had been denied the chance to offer my testimony that Russell couldn't have been the one to fire the shots – he was with me at the time. He wanted to take all the blame.

Besotted. I hadn't guessed Henri even knew of such a word. As to whether I ever tried hard enough to insist that the truth as I knew it to be must be heard, no matter what Russell or anybody else said – only my conscience could tell me that, and it has never chosen to do so clearly. And, yes – I think it very probable I haven't wanted it to.

Seventeen

I

There was nothing much more on his screen. The narrative ended there. A few notes and headings followed, set down to jog his memory whenever he should return to the task. He did not think that was likely to happen now. He had failed, he knew it. He had set out to write his wife's obituary, and thousands of words had not brought him even close to the meat of the story. Except for a few scattered references, mostly to his own disastrous sexual adventure during it, he had barely touched on the history of her parliamentary years, a time in which, briefly, she had seemed to sway a little the destinies of the nation. 'Stabler Defection Brings SDP Government "That Much Closer" ', a broadsheet headline of the day had proclaimed, quoting an unnamed source. The source in fact had been Vincent; nevertheless, there had been in those few days and weeks a real sense of destiny in the air. Never felt before, by either the Stablers or their new Party; never to be recaptured. But it had been there, once. And he had failed really to get it down.

He went over the final notes a last time. Mostly even these, he saw, referred to Russell's story rather than Bubbles'. Standing trial for the fairground incident. The lies and fictions emitted by a parade of police witnesses. The appearance of Ivor Trasker as an expert witness for the prosecution to testify to Russell's central role in the South London criminal fraternity (getting his own back, and a bit more, for all Russell's scorn and disrespect towards his precious study over the weeks it was going on). The judge's summing-up was harsh: 'Few crimes can be more contemptible or serious than to take deliberate aim at a defenceless mother and child.' The five years he gave Russell were the 'very least the defendant could expect in the circumstances'. Word from Goldy via Russell's brief that if he kept quiet about Val's involvement, then his family would be 'taken care of'. The rumours in the constituency that the whole thing had been a police stitch-up. The indignation. A desire to show the authorities that the people would have a representative of their own choosing no matter what.

It was like John Wilkes in the Middlesex election long ago. And perhaps Wilkes too had had somebody like Goldy in the background, bribing, threatening, cajoling, steering the party the right way. Poor Jack Rolls, who had thought his time had come at last, was persuaded to stand aside (a second time, if his shade was to be believed). A packed and sympathetic selection meeting chose Bubbles to stand in her husband's stead in the general election that was expected sometime next year. A grateful letter from Russell in Wandsworth prison was read to the meeting. Great applause. Ironically it was Baz Jacobson, then in his romantic Marxist phase, who had led the call for Bubbles to be chosen. He had been very keen on Russell, and wanted to show his admiration the best way he could.

'Between the bloody Stablers and Baz sodding Jacobson

you lot turned this place into fucking Alabama,' Jack Rolls had grumbled to Vincent at some time during his later, drunken, malevolent period. 'Or Mississippi. The governor's wife taking over from the governor when he dies – what a disgrace. How un-English!'

'Russell didn't die,' Vincent had pointed out.

'Might as well have done. How long did he get for that guard? Thirty years?'

'Twenty. He only served sixteen of that sentence.'

Only sixteen. There was a hit song of that name in Vincent's teenage years. Referred to the extreme youth of the girl who was being serenaded. But sixteen years in prison? No 'only' about that; it was a hell of a stretch. With what remained of the original sentence, it meant that Russell was out of circulation for nearly nineteen years. Nine months into his first sentence, he had assaulted a prison guard. The man had died seven weeks later. At his second trial, his lawyer had worked hard to establish that the assault and the death had had little to do with each other. The jury was not convinced. What never came out was that Russell had made the attack – so out of character, as even the other guards were forced to admit from the witness stand – in the midst of his grief and fury at the news that his wife and his younger brother, who had worked so hard on her behalf during her recent successful election campaign, were now cohabiting. (The news had arrived at Russell's cell courtesy of Goldy, a piece of meanness that was also, Vincent thought, quite out of character.)

If Russell had spilled the beans here, told the court of the intolerable strains he had been under, it might have gone a little way towards mitigating his crime. That he did not was received by Bubbles and Vincent with natural if somewhat craven relief. Not long into her parliamentary career, she had just heard a distant (and, it turned out, unreliable) rumour that somebody might be interested in taking her on as his parliamentary private secretary. Messy publicity now would have certainly set back her chances.

'It never rains but it pours.' Actually one of Vincent and Russell's mother's favourite catchphrases or sayings. She was not spared the news of her oldest son's latest and gravest offence. She sat in court every day during the trial. The prisoner smiled at her whenever he entered or left the courtroom. Vincent was not there to witness these moments; he read about them in the papers. The Monster of Black-heath grinning defiantly in the dock. It was like the old days; the placards were everywhere proclaiming Russell's crimes. Luckily their father did not have to face anew the dilemma of whether or not to exhibit them outside his shop. Between Russell's first and second offences, he had died and the shop had been sold, lock, stock and goodwill.

II

The afternoon drifted away. The early dusk of November showed outside Vincent's window. He sat in front of his monitor, scrolling again through his text. Occasionally he made a change in the wording, or corrected a fact. Mostly he still felt that he'd failed Bubbles. Not got her right, not got her at all really. Several times the sense of failure was so strong that he selected all the text and his finger hovered over the delete key. Each time so far he had held back, but it would have to go eventually, he sensed.

Once he left the study to go into the kitchen to make himself a cup of tea. At first he was glad to be out of the little room: it was indeed so little, and had grown so stuffy from his presence and from the humming warmth of the computer. But a sudden assault from Rodney (in alliance with Guns'n'Roses) soon drove him back. It was ridiculous, he fumed, as again he selected the whole text, nobody should have to live like this, and since Rodney couldn't or wouldn't change his habits, Vincent would have to go. Which would be no hardship certainly; in fact he'd be glad of it. He would have put the idea to Bubbles months ago, except that months ago it was already out of the question, she could not have stood a move.

What did he feel now? Exhausted. Numb. Blank. Glad that the day was over, that for sure, but most of all – yes, *exhausted*. He drooped forward in his seat. His forehead briefly touched the keyboard. He'd forgotten that he had selected all the text. When he looked up, it was all gone. Thousands and thousands of words vanished entirely. He must have pressed 'delete' with his head. Perhaps it was for the best.

He heard a taxi draw up in the road. He looked at the window. It was black night outside now. How late was it? He heard footsteps in the streets, the only noise in a silent world. Even in this room, the faintest murmurs of Rodney's music got through. But there was nothing now at all. He waited, staring at the empty screen.

The doorbell brought him out of his chair. Down the stairs, slowly. He had got out of the habit of answering the front door outside those times when he was expecting the doctor or somebody from the hospice. Other than they, it was almost always some bugger trying to sell him something. Or one of Rodney's friends who had pressed the wrong bell by mistake. Either way he had no interest in sorting out their needs. Genuine visitors – the one or two per month – would always phone ahead.

It was too late for a salesman or a missionary. If it was one of Rodney's chums . . .

It wasn't.

'You don't look that surprised, Vincent,' he said.

'I'm not. I heard you'd set your heart on it.'

'You busy?'

'I was working on the computer. Had an accident. Lost the entire file.'

'Too bad.'

'No problem. I just remembered I've got almost all of it on a floppy . . . Where are the boys?'

'We took Rob out to the airport. I dropped the other lad back at the hotel.'

'Are you going to beat me up, Russell?'

'Have a heart. I've got blood-pressure.'

Vincent nodded. 'Right.' He opened the door wide. 'Well, you'd better come in, hadn't you?'

III

That night Jack Rolls did his best to have the last word. He struck at just gone quarter past four in the morning, probably hoping to find Vincent too befuddled to present

232

much opposition. But after the last weeks with Bubbles, such hours posed no threat to Vincent any more. He had the light on, he was ready, waiting, staring at the ceiling. The phone was at his ear, his glasses on his nose, almost before its first ring was completed.

'Tough luck, Jack. Your tactic failed. I'm as awake as – As awake as—'

'You can't think of the word, can you? Try lark.'

'*Lark*?'

'This is getting us nowhere. How was Russell? Changed much?'

'I suppose so. He's put on quite a lot of weight. I noticed he wheezed quite badly on the stairs. Well, poor old fellow – he's sixty now, very nearly.'

'So are you nearly.'

'And not much hair any more. It used to be so full and black and glossy—'

'You don't have to tell me. I knew Russell then. In fact he ruined my life for me, so I remember him quite well. Him and his hair. When I asked you how Russell was, I didn't mean just his appearance. Though I'm sure that comprises your entire measure of a man, you vain ass, Stabler. I meant – was *he* changed? In himself?'

'How can I tell that?'

'You sat and talked to him for . . . how long?'

'Maybe an hour. By the end we were both looking at our watches.'

'You didn't have much to say to each other?'

'Not much. It was sort of desultory. I thanked him for coming to the service. And the reception.'

'Yes, it was nice that one of her husbands could do the decent thing.'

'Mostly we talked about the boys. Well, about Rob. I told him early on I didn't have anything good to say about Tim.'

'And?'

'It didn't bother him. He said he'd always told Tim he should go see his mum, but he just refused . . . It was a delicate area. We didn't linger on it. He talked about being in business now with Tim. The boy quit teaching, we knew that. Married some girl, Rachel, Rob showed us a picture of her once, pretty girl . . . Anyway, Russell and Tim, they hire out stuff. Things like . . . buzz-saws and long ladders and – I don't know – things people wouldn't actually own. Says they're doing quite well. Shop's just outside Coventry. They have plans to open another in Nuneaton.' Vincent chuckled. 'You know, Jack, listening to him reminded me so much of our father. He always had these expansionary plans. He wanted to be able to talk about, you know: "Our Crystal Palace branch", "Our Streatham branch", "Our Beckenham headquarters". Weekends he and my mother would always be going out in the old Morris van, looking over likely—'

Vincent's reminiscences were cut off at this point by a stagy yawn down the phone.

'So, the great reunion – bit of a flop, was it?'

'There was one interesting thing came up.'

'One in an hour? That's—'

'Shut up, Jack. Listen to this . . . Remember that when the police and the crowd went after Russell and Val on the heath, it was because a woman had pointed them out? And

234

had told the police that Russell had been the shooter? A mystery woman – never found afterwards?'

'I remember.'

'It was Bubbles. Val saw her talking to a cop. She'd been following them around the fairground. They'd seen her earlier. That's why Val and Russell separated that night, and he came over to the dodgems. Because of Bubbles.'

'I thought she was in Bromley that evening. At her mum's?'

'It's five miles from Blackheath. Less. She had the car. She could have left the boys with her mother, got over there easy.'

'So she fingered them? And lied about Russell?'

'According to Russell. Val told him that night. He was getting her out of the back of the factory, just ahead of the cops. Your fucking wife, she was screaming, she did it! He never saw Val again. I told him what I knew. How she went to Spain, that she might still be out there. It didn't seem to interest him. It's all in the past as far as he's concerned.'

'Do you believe it's true about Bubbles? D'you think she could be so – vicious?'

'Bubbles jealous? I think she would be capable of almost anything. I've seen her in that state, don't forget.'

'Thanks for reminding me, Stabler.'

'I told Russell I didn't believe it. Said Val probably made it up, out of spite. That it was the sort of thing I could see her doing.'

'Is that what you really think?'

'Not sure.'

'Is Russell angry?'

'With Bubbles? Not any more. He says she would have gone to the police, told 'em what had really happened, but he didn't want her to.'

'Because of Val?'

'Because of Val . . . Anyway he says it wasn't Bubbles who put him in jail. That was between him and the police, and the lies they told the jury. But even there, he doesn't blame them much. He'd been untouchable for so long and he could see why they could hardly let him go once they got a chance at him. By the way, did I tell you he married a second time in jail? We'd heard about that. Name of Penny. Prison visitor. They're still together. But look—'

'Look, what?'

'What if it's true? What if Bubbles did finger them?'

'Well, what if?'

'Twenty-five years we were together, and she never told me *that*?'

'And?'

'And so what else didn't she tell me?'

IV

Jack seemed to take a lot of time to consider the question. At least when Vincent became aware again of the phone in his hand, it was dawn outside, early dawn. The traveller's clock said ten to six. He thought Jack must surely have hung up by now, but even as he started to enquire about it, he heard the familiar voice out of the ear-piece. He pressed it closer against his head.

'What did you say, Jack?'

'I said: here you are, Vincent. Alone. Pretty well unemployed . . . Though no change there, I suppose. You haven't really ever had a job, have you? Except for when you were Bubbles' gofer.'

'Excuse me? Political adviser? Right-hand man? Amanuensis?'

'Whatever.'

'And you're forgetting when I used to be a college lecturer.'

'Best if that stayed forgotten . . . But seriously: no particular skills, and the wrong side of fifty-five. Where do you go from here?'

Vincent hesitated.

'I can see that's floored you,' Jack sniggered.

'Actually – I was considering my options. The thing about Bubbles' death,' Vincent went on (he felt himself, as he often did nowadays, hovering between brilliant insights and crass foolishness), 'is that, regrettable as it is, it does open up certain possibilities. You know, one door closes, another swings open. That kind of thing. And the fact is we were in pretty much of a rut, her and me: a cocoa-drinking, TV-watching, where's-the-bickies? kind of a rut. Could have gone on till we'd both dropped dead of old age. It needed something pretty big to blast us out of it. So it was a bit of luck in a way, what happened.'

'You're a heartless bastard, aren't you, Stabler?'

'I know. I'll hate myself for saying this tomorrow. Tomorrow I'm going to pretend I never said it – though this is tomorrow now, isn't it?'

'And you're wrong. You'll still be in a rut. And you'll be even poorer than you are now. She was the bread-winner, wasn't she? You just won't be in a cocoa-and-bickies rut. Because you won't be able to afford them.'

'Actually, I don't think I'll be any worse off, maybe even a bit better. Bubbles was always religious about keeping up her life insurance premiums. I told her it was a waste of money, we should enjoy it while we were still fairly young. But she would go and write those cheques every year. Not much each one, but they added up.'

'Then – what are you saying? Are you a millionaire now?'

'Don't be ridiculous. I shall just have a bit coming in every month. I shan't have to worry really. And maybe I'll do some more lectures, I've had offers. Maybe I'll still put in a day or two a week at the picture library. But I plan to take a holiday before I figure all that out.'

'To where? The USA?'

'. . . Why do you say that?'

'To find your daughter of course. She's probably still over there, isn't she? If she's still alive.'

'Of course she's alive. Her mother would have told me if anything bad had happened. Matty MacBride is not a monster.'

'That's a change of tune.'

'Well, she isn't any more. Also I have to face the fact that what happened between us certainly wasn't only her fault. Mistakes on both sides, I'm prepared to admit.'

'Big of you.'

'And then we were so young when we broke up. *She* was

still almost a teenager, for God's sake. Plus, she was disoriented. My God, *I* was disoriented at Cambridge, and I'm English . . . Anyway, she's doing fine now. Married this guy, used to be a hip record producer in the old days. One of those people who got on the cover of *Rolling Stone*? Now he's some sort of conglomerate. TV. Music. Oil. An ice-hockey team. She works with him. Runs one of the company's divisions. A home-shopping channel, I think. Oh yes, Matty's doing great.'

'You're in touch with her then?'

'A bit . . . I was told when Ellen got her doctorate from Stanford last year for instance.'

'Ellen?'

'Ellen. My daughter.'

'So you could easily find her?'

'. . . I've thought about it.'

'And?'

'I've thought about it . . . Why would Ellen want to meet me? After all these years?'

'Ah, don't be a coward, Vincent.'

They sat in companionable silence at either end of the phone. He heard Jack yawn, felt like doing the same. He could go back to sleep. There was nothing to get up for. His dear wife was dead and buried. Or rather her ashes were due for collection from the undertaker's. He had said he'd be in to pick up the casket tomorrow. Today, that is. But there was no hurry, if he didn't feel like it. And he had no strong desire to be awake. Asleep he could pretend to be brave in the face of his loss. Awake he knew it would not be easy. It would be just hell pretty often, he knew. Like Russell contemplating splitting from Val a quarter of a century ago. Just like hell. He had no relish for facing that.

'And so,' Jack sighed at last, 'Russell came – and then Russell went.'

'That's it. I think he was just curious to see how I was. And curiosity satisfied – he went away. We shook hands. Didn't make any plans for another meeting. I didn't even bother to go down the stairs to see him out.'

'And that was it.'

'Mm. Except for one curious thing. Rather sad than curious really. You see, just before he left, Rodney's music started up again. Really loud, we could hardly hear ourselves speak. I explained where and who it was coming from. Russell said, "This is just not on." He said he'd have a talk with Rodney on his way out. And I thought, that's it, I will never have to hear another note of that fucking awful music as long as I live. I still had such automatic faith in Russell. My big brother. What he said went. He would put the frighteners on Rodney, and that would be it forever, like magic.'

'So?'

'So when he'd gone, I heard him downstairs knocking on Rodney's door. Few muffled words. A moment or two and – sure enough – the music went off. Nothing. Silence. Fabulous. Russell had done it.'

'For ever?'

'Twenty minutes later, the music was back. Loud as before, louder, went on till past midnight. Rodney didn't give a stuff for Russell. He was just another old geezer on the moan. Russell's magic is gone.'

'That sounds like the envious little brother, climbing to the top of the family dungheap at last.'

'No,' said Vincent, after thinking it over, 'it wasn't like that. It was a good thing. A healthy thing. One more sign that the past is over. Done with.'

'And Vincent will move on now? Relentlessly!'

'I know why you're sneering, Jack. Because it wasn't your way, was it? Your way was to hit a brick wall and then sit on the ground bawling drunkenly about it for your last fifteen years on earth.'

'Aren't you a charmer, Vincent.'

'I'm not like you, that's for sure. And when it comes to such matters as moving on, there's another difference between us which may have the potential to influence and shape our separate points of view.'

'Spoken like a failed academic. What difference would that be, Vincent?'

'You're dead,' shouted Vincent exultantly, and he slammed down the phone, depriving Jack of any chance at all at the vital last word.

Eighteen

Milestones

Anthea Jean Stabler (neé Hopkins), born 7 January 1946 at South View Nursing Home in Bromley, Kent; died 9 November 1998 at home in Norbury, South London, after a long illness, bravely borne.

For just over nine years Anthea Stabler was a Member of Parliament, first in the Labour interest, then, after her resignation from that party, in that of the Social Democrats. Particularly in the weeks around her resignation from Labour, she had been something of a celebrity. Her photograph appeared in the newspapers, she was asked to speak on radio and TV. She had enjoyed the fuss, and the sense of importance, and her brief period of fame, and in fact had been grateful for her whole time as an MP – yet she'd never been able to make her second husband understand that she did not regard these as the most important experiences of her life.

Her moment of greatest happiness had been when her first son had come back to her. Her greatest grief had been that her second son had left her for ever (followed closely by her prolonged despair over her second husband's infidelity in 1982 with Audrey Angela Rolls, neé Destefano). Her most passionate times had been in the early months of her first marriage when she had felt sometimes such longing for her husband's body that if he was not there to hold her it brought on radiant flushes all over her body, she couldn't breathe, she sweated so much it soaked her clothes. This happened at work a couple of times, and her fellow employees at Chiesemans of Lewisham became alarmed at the spectacle and urged her to go to the in-store sanatorium and lie down. Which made her laugh because she did indeed so much want to lie down, but only in her Russell's arms.

And the times of her greatest contentment had been in her second marriage, beginning a year or so after the 1983 election, when they were out in the cold, just the two of them. She no longer hated Vincent because of his unfaithfulness. She had thought she never would get over it. Her hurt went on and on. It felt like it would ruin her whole life if it didn't stop. As a last desperate throw, she decided to find out if it would help at all if she evened up the score. She got in contact with a former parliamentary colleague, Malcolm Worthington, who had also recently lost his seat. Malcolm was at a bit of a loose end, not wanting to go back North, hanging around London without a real job. He was delighted to get her call. Of course she knew he'd always had a bit of a crush on her. Over lunch at Bianchi's in Soho, she established that the flame still flickered. (He seemed not at all put off by her recent weight-gain: 'All the more of you to adore,' he had toasted her gallantly.) Their affair, conducted mostly at Malcolm's shabby little flat in Stoke Newington, lasted three months, until the offer of a job in New York took him away from her. It didn't bother her much to see him go. The sex had been quite satisfactory, but as far his company went, Malcolm the boyfriend had proved easily as boring as plain Malcolm the colleague.

But best of all, she found that her real reason for entering the affair had been justified. Her feelings towards Vincent had undergone a sea-change. It helped that his behaviour ever since Audrey bloody Rolls had blabbed all the details of their tryst had been abject and apologetic to the point of hang-dog. But essentially she could let go at last of the violence of her rancour because she could regard him now with pity, as a victim himself. (Even though an unwitting one, for of course she never divulged to him what she was really doing all those afternoons when, as he thought, she had been fulfilling last-minute bookings from Terry Farquarson.) She still wished the Audrey business had never happened. But it had. No sense prolonging the agony. She forgave Vincent, she took him back into her arms. And she began to eat even more massively than before.

This – her growing portliness, and then her actual arrival at obesity – was the only real cloud over the last fifteen years of her life. She kept herself busy with the lectures and the housekeeping, and listening to Classic FM by day and watching TV at night and worrying about Rob in Ireland and mourning over Tim in whichever new Midlands town she'd most recently discovered he'd moved to. And with loving Vincent. It was a source of wonder even to her sometimes how much she loved him.

'You can't ever feel for me as much as you did for Russell,' he would say. And she would reply I do, I do. And she did. Even when she remembered, with a deep-down twinge, how she had craved so much once to be entered by the other brother, her conviction did not waver. Vincent, she knew, was by far the lesser man; yet with him she had been fifty times happier. They fitted. He was the love of her life. Towards the end she even convinced him of it.

Anthea Jean Hopkins/Stabler/Stabler. 'Bubbles'. Born in the first half of the twentieth century, she did not quite make it out of the second. She had not been chosen to help take the space-ship into the next millennium. Her name would not be on that roster. Still she had done her bit to get the vessel this far, and had left behind among the crew of billions a few more-or-less willing hands who, with any luck, would be able to carry the work on for a good few years yet: namely her widower Vincent, her ex-husband Russell who, from jealousy, she had cruelly wronged, her sons Rob and Tim, her daughter-in-law Rachel Stabler and, though she did not know it at her death, her grandchildren Steven Russell and Carly Anthea, twins, who had recently taken up residence in Rachel's womb.

A NOTE ON THE TYPE

This old style face is named after the Frenchman
Robert Granjon, a sixteenth-century letter cutter
whose italic types have often been used with the
romans of Claude Garamond. The origins of this
face, like those of Garamond, lie in the late
fifteenth-century types used by Aldus Manutius
in Italy. A good face for setting text in books,
magazines and periodicals.